GIRL OVERBOARD!

Heartlines

Books by Pam Lyons

A Boy Called Simon
He Was Bad
It Could Never Be
Latchkey Girl
Danny's Girl
Odd Girl Out
Ms Perfect
One of the Boys

Books by Anita Eires

Tug of Love
Summer Awakening
Spanish Exchange
Star Dreamer
Californian Summer
If Only . . .
Teacher's Pet
Working Girl

Books by Mary Hooper

Love Emma XXX
Follow That Dream
My Cousin Angie
Happy Ever After
Opposites Attract
A Love Like Yours

Books by Barbara Jacobs

Two Times Two

Books by Jane Pitt

Loretta Rose
Autumn Always Comes
Stony Limits
Rainbows For Sale
Pia

Books by Ann de Gale

Island Encounter
Hands Off

Books by Anthea Cohen

Dangerous Love

Books by David S Williams

Give Me Back My Pride
Forgive and Forget

Books by Jill Young

Change Of Heart
Three Summers On

Books by Ann Ruffell

Friends For Keeps
Secret Passion
Baby Face

Books by Lorna Read

Images
The Name Is Zero

Books by Jane Butterworth

Spotlight On Sam

Books by John Harvey

Wild Love

Books by Anita Davies

Stepsisters

heartlines

Pam Lyons

Girl Overboard!

A Pan Original

My thanks to Lee and Dan for their help in chartering my course!

First published 1988 by Pan Books Ltd
Cavaye Place, London SW10 9PG
9 8 7 6 5 4 3 2 1
© Pam Lyons 1988
ISBN 0 330 30077 6

Printed and bound in Great Britain by
Richard Clay Ltd, Bungay, Suffolk

Chapter 1

It was hot. Very hot. I dropped my bulging hold-all on the concrete and let out an exasperated sigh before turning to confront Kevin.

'So where to now, big brother?' I asked. Drops of perspiration were trickling down the back of my neck, and my sweatshirt, adequate for the icy blasts of England, was now sticking to my damp skin.

Kevin, ever the optimist, for once looked perplexed.

'Well, the bar must be somewhere along here. Kim and Roger said it was in the Port of Andraitx. And this is the Port of Andraitx. Look,' he said, 'let's just sit over at one of those quayside tables and have a cold drink. Then we'll ask someone.'

'How's your Spanish?'

He ignored my question. 'Don't be daft, Sue. This is one of the most famous Mediterranean harbours in the world. It'll be bursting with cosmopolitan people. Someone's bound to know English.'

'Let's hope you're right!' I bent to lift my Adidas and began to follow him. 'Hey,' I called, 'don't they speak Mallorquin here, not Spanish?'

'What's the odds?' Kevin had reached an empty table and dumped his nylon hold-all and rucksack on a spare chair. 'We don't speak either, right?' He sank down on a low-slung, cane chair, then stretched his long, jean-covered legs out in front of him – almost tripping me up.

'Watch out, stupid,' I mumbled, bad-humouredly. 'That's all I need before our working holiday begins – a sprained ankle. A great help I'll be crewing on the *Golden Goddess* with one foot in plaster.'

Grinning, Kevin leaned over and tugged my long hair which I'd tied to one side in a ponytail.

'Stop that!' I pulled away from him, then began to glance about us. If I hadn't felt so hot, tired and irritable, I'd probably have been enchanted by the view. As it was, the old fishing port and its natural harbour, the incredibly aquamarine sea and deeper blue sky made only a passing impression. The fact was, I needed both a toilet and a long, cold drink – in that order.

'Where are you off to?' Kevin asked surprised, as I jumped up and started to cross the dusty road towards a row of stone houses and restaurants opposite.

'Don't ask!' I pulled a face. 'If a waiter comes, I'd like something cold and long, with lots of ice.'

'If you're going where I think you're going, find out where the men's are, too, will you?'

I didn't answer. I was too busy playing hopscotch with a darkly suntanned boy on a moped who'd decided to stop suddenly right in my path.

'Watch out!' I said. As I started to walk round him the engine of his bike spluttered, then cut out.

'Thanks a million!' the boy blazed.

6

I was so startled by his outburst – and in English, too – that my immediate need was momentarily forgotten.

'What do you mean, "thanks a million"? It was your fault. You were so busy giving those two girls the once-over that you weren't looking where you were going.'

The stranger's dark eyes flashed dangerously. 'Rubbish' he retorted. 'It's obvious you're a stranger here, otherwise you'd have looked in the right direction. We drive on the right in Spain. And this part of the road's one-way. And if you want to live to be fifteen, I suggest you learn that fast.'

'I'm seventeen *actually*,' I stormed, the heat and my temper meeting melting point. 'And I *was* looking the right way.'

'In which case,' the boy said, sardonically, 'you're old enough to have road sense, and you probably need glasses. Now, if you don't mind, some of us aren't on holiday.'

He kicked the engine back to life and roared off towards the far end of the quay.

I might have continued standing there, fuming, if the angry hooting of a car hadn't propelled me across the street and into the dark, almost dank, interior of the nearest cafe.

The sudden change from glaring midday sunlight to almost blackness made it difficult for me to focus for a few seconds. When my eyes grew accustomed to my dim surroundings, I glanced around hopefully.

'If you need the *services*, they are behind the bar – over there,' a woman with bleached, curly hair said in faltering English. She pointed, cloth in hand, towards a dark corner.

I smiled my thanks, then hurriedly made my way across to the archway she had pointed to. In faded lettering above it, I could just make out the word she had spoken.

A few minutes later, I walked out into the bright sunshine feeling a whole lot better. Making a point of looking carefully before crossing the road, I ran across and flopped down on the chair opposite Kevin.

'Not the best loos in the world, but they are clean,' I informed him, as I leaned forward and gratefully took the tall glass of lemonade he handed me.

Kevin clinked his glass against mine, making the stack of ice-cubes jangle.

'Cheers, big-ears!' he toasted me, using the familiar tease which normally made me mad.

For once, I refused to be baited. 'Cheers!' I replied. I sipped a long, thirst-quenching mouthful of the fizzy drink before relaxing back in my seat. 'Mmm,' I breathed, closing my eyes and feeling the sun hot on my face, 'this is the life.'

'Who was the tall, dark, handsome stranger?' Kevin asked.

I opened one eye and squinted over the top of my glass at him. 'You heard?'

My brother nodded, and laughed shortly. 'Quite a pantomime, wasn't it? Mind you, sis, he was right. You didn't look in the right direction.'

I opened my other eye. 'You want an argument the first day we arrive in Mallorca?'

Kevin scowled and shook his mop of thick, fair hair.

I placed my lips round my straw and continued to sip, enjoying the feel of the cold fizz against my tongue. The glass, under my fingers, was wet and cold. I placed it against my hot cheek.

'What I wouldn't give for a nice refreshing swim right now,' Kevin said, gazing out across the harbour to the glinting, sparkling water beyond the sea wall. He let out a deep sigh, finished his drink, then stood up.

'I'll go pay the bill, then find out where Donal's Bar is.'

I nodded, feeling suddenly relaxed and lazy and not caring that we were basically lost, in a strange land, with nowhere to sleep. It all seemed suddenly unimportant.

I watched Kevin cross the road, then let my eyes wander along the large, beautiful outer and inner harbours, where the moorings were filled with every type of boat you could imagine. Their paintwork and fittings flashed, diamond-bright in the noonday heat. Close by, a few seagulls circled lazily on the air currents near a group of fishing trawlers: further out, to the north, the squat outline of the club house was just visible, shimmering at the edge of the turquoise water.

At least, I assumed it was the club house, because it fitted the location and description we'd been given.

Near the club, I could see an area of hard standing and the stark, almost toylike outline of a small crane.

Somewhere out there, I thought, lazily, scanning

the array of masts and furled sails, jewel-like chrome and brightly-coloured hulls that sat for all the world like a collection of exotic birds on the calm water, is the *Golden Goddess*.

Just the name of the sixty-three-foot motor-sailer conjured up unbelievable pictures of luxury and adventure.

It was a world away from the sea-front at Burnham-on-Crouch, where we lived. Even on a good day, the Atlantic was never as clear as the Mediterranean; the sky never as blue. And although I loved our home town, now, compared to the muted ochre and mellowed stones of the waterfront houses, each with their olive-green shutters and sun-bleached awnings, it was like comparing an old black-and-white to a brilliantly-coloured movie. There just wasn't any comparison.

How could I have ever been apprehensive about coming here? I wondered, dreamily, breathing in the tangy, salt-laden air. My eyes darted from one pretty scene to another. The colours were all so vibrant and clear in the searing sunlight. It was incredible. I nearly laughed, now, as I recalled my reaction when Roger Carter, the owner of our local sailing school, had first suggested the idea to Mum and Dad.

'Don't look so frightened, Susan,' Roger had said, noticing my expression, 'there's really nothing to it. You and Kevin are both excellent sailors – else there's no way I'd allow you to teach the youngsters at my sailing school.'

Dad, who'd spent his life messing around on boats,

was very enthusiastic. 'So,' he'd recapped, 'Kevin and Sue crew for your friends on their ship the *Golden Goddess* round the Balearic islands *and* get paid? Phew! Sounds like an opportunity of a lifetime.'

Kim, Roger's wife and partner at the sailing school had smiled at me, reassuringly. 'You wouldn't be the only crew, Sue, pet,' she explained. 'Rosie and José love sailing so much they accompany every charter on the *Golden Goddess*. And it's not as if he's chartering the boat to strangers. They are usually old friends, or friends of friends who hire the boat.'

Mum, who had never been a keen sailor, hadn't looked too happy. Kevin, however, had grown really excited at the idea.

Kevin, I should explain, has also inherited Dad's love of the sea, like me. We're never happier than when we are down at the sailing club helping out, or sailing with Dad in his small dinghy. It's a fabulous hobby – even if the weather round the east coast of England is so unpredictable.

'The *Golden Goddess* is a beautiful motor-sailer,' Kim had gone on to explain. 'And our great friends Rosie and José are reliable as well as first-class sailors. We've often talked about Sue and Kevin, and now your kids are old enough, it seems a lovely opportunity for them to see a bit of the world as well as fulfilling every boat owner's dream of cruising the Med. They'd be in good hands, Fay,' she'd added, mostly, I'd thought, for Mum's peace of mind.

But Mum hadn't been convinced.

Dad, on the other hand, had taken up our cause with gusto.

'And you say these friends charter every summer?'

Roger had nodded. 'For six weeks in the summer – the rest Rosie and José have for themselves. In August they usually take the boat across to the North coast of Africa – just a family affair.'

Dad's bright blue eyes – which Kevin and I inherited along with his love of the sea – literally sparkled.

'Sounds like my idea of Heaven,' he mused. 'Maybe one day, when the kids are off our hands, we'll sell up, invest in a good boat and just sail off into the sunset, eh Fay?'

I'd glanced across the table at Mum. From the set of her mouth, I knew she hadn't been thinking along the same lines as Dad. Mum and the sea just didn't mix.

Mum had caught my eye. 'What about you, Sue? Do you like the idea?'

I had had to admit that I did. 'The only problem is, am I capable of working such a boat? Crewing for Dad's one thing – but the *Golden Goddess* sounds pretty formidable. Almost like crewing on the *Q.E.II!*'

But when Kim had then explained my job wouldn't be so much crewing as helping out with any youngsters who came with their parents for charters, I okayed the idea.

'Hey – stop dreaming, kiddo, we'd better make tracks,' Kevin said, interrupting my reverie.

I wiped a trickle of perspiration off my cheek and

pushed the sleeves of my thick sweatshirt up to my elbows.

'Where are we making tracks to?' I asked, reaching for my hold-all.

Kevin pointed to the far side of the bay. 'Over there, so the waiter told me. Donal's Bar is almost opposite, across the water.'

I looked at the large circular bay, and at the distance ahead of us. 'Come on, Kev! We can't walk that distance in this heat. I'll melt.'

Kevin wasn't sympathetic. 'Well, you could try swimming,' he suggested.

'Fun-ny! Isn't there a bus, or taxi we can take?'

'Nope,' came the quick reply. 'No buses go round the causeway, and the only taxi's on its way to the airport. So, it's walk – or walk. Make your choice.'

'Oh, in that case,' I replied, 'I think I'll walk.' With that, I picked up my bag, hitched it over my shoulder and strode ahead of him.

Kevin hesitated long enough to leave a tip of a few pesetas, before he ran to catch up, matching his long stride to mine. At five foot seven I was almost as tall as him and Dad, and Mum swears my legs are longer than any of theirs. Now, refreshed from the lemonade and beginning to grow accustomed to the heat unusual for the middle of June, I found a spring in my step that hadn't been there earlier.

'Isn't it fantastic?' I said, making a wide sweep with my free arm of the bay and distant, craggy, pine-covered mountains. 'Smell that glorious sea air.'

Kevin plodded on, not bothering to look at me. 'Keep your eulogizing for later, will you, Sue? Let's see how we get on after a few days. That's supposing we ever find Rosie and José, not to mention the phantom ship.'

'Don't be so miserable, Kev. Of course we'll find them and it. All we've got to do is find Donal's Bar and ask there, that's simple.' I started humming a tune as we turned off left from the quay and began walking along the causeway towards the far side of the bay.

We hadn't walked far when my eye caught sight of a beautiful meandering waterway, off to the right.

'Just look at that, will you, Kev?' I called. 'Isn't that something? It's like one of those famous French paintings with all those small, colourful boats moored bow to stern. Oh, stop, do! I want to take a photo to show Mum and Dad when we get back.'

'Not now,' Kevin called over his shoulder. 'We've got six weeks to take photos. Let's find the boat first.'

I ignored him. I love my brother but sometimes his sense of timing's all out. Without saying another word I dashed across the narrow roadway and unzippered my hold-all. My Polaroid was right on the top where I'd put it after taking photos of Palma airport, when we arrived. The pictures I'd already taken had come out beautifully — one of the joys of a Polaroid. Anyway, I can't bear waiting for anything — let alone pictures I've taken. I always want to see immediately that they've come out all right. I mean, what's the point of going all the way back home, waiting for them to be developed at the chemist's — then discovering you were out of focus, or you had your thumb stuck over the lens?

I took two of the waterway – one straight on. The other at an angle with a few tall reeds in the foreground, for the artistic effect.

I waited for the film to develop, then smiled happily. They were super.

'Hey, Kevin!' I called. 'Hang on, will you? You wait till you see these pictures. They're really professional.'

Without thinking, I darted out to cross the road just as Kevin turned. The expression on his face suddenly changed from exasperation to fear.

My name came to his lips but I didn't hear him call out because at that precise moment there was a screeching of tyres ... a scrunch of gravel and a dull, heavy thud. Followed immediately by some very guttural and not very nice swear words.

I swung round to see what all the commotion was about – and I saw *him*. The same deeply-tanned, curly-headed boy who had been so rude to me earlier. Only this time, he was horizontal, not vertical. And so was his moped.

'You!' he spat out, wiping the dust and grime from his face.

I didn't know whether to smile, or be quiet. I half stepped towards him, to help him to his feet, but he made it quite plain he didn't want my help.

'You're a menace to traffic.' The boy glowered in my direction as he tried to get up. I could see from his expression and pale tightened lips that he was in pain. 'You are dangerous, you know that?'

Kevin reached him and began helping the boy to his feet.

'We're so sorry,' my brother was apologizing. 'I'm afraid my sister Sue wasn't thinking—'

'Is she capable of thinking?' Two dark eyes flashed furiously in my direction. Then a peculiar thing happened. As the boy began to dust the dirt off his now far from clean shorts, he stopped, and stood upright.

'Did you say – your sister, Sue?' There was a thinness to his voice – as if the answer might cause him more pain.

Kevin glanced across, clearly puzzled, like me. 'That's right,' he said, 'Why?'

A grazed and grimy hand shot to the stranger's brow. A look of what I could only describe as shock contorted his face.

'Don't tell me? And you're Kevin, right?'

Kevin nodded, two lines now creasing his brow. 'That's right. Should we know you?'

The fingers raked the thick black curls, and a set expression tightened the boy's lips.

'Well, isn't that just my luck?' He was shaking his head, a look of disbelief tinged with sardonic amusement on his face. From beneath lowered thick lashes, I felt his eyes assessing me – from my ponytail, down to my canvas-soled sailing shoes.

'Look, would you like to let us in on your amusing secret?' Kevin's voice was sharp.

The expression on the boy's face eased a bit. The next second he shot out a hand to Kevin.

'I'm Alejandro Covas,' he announced. 'Alex, for short.'

Kevin took the proffered hand and shook it politely. But, like me, he still looked confused.

'Are you from Donal's Bar, by any chance?' Kevin asked, hopefully.

'No,' came the reply. Then to our amazement, Alejandro said, 'I'm from the *Golden Goddess*. I'm the son of Rosie and José Covas. It seems we're to be shipmates for the next six weeks.'

At that precise moment, I willed the hot, dusty, Mallorquin road beneath my size six feet to open up and swallow me.

Chapter 2

'If you're as clumsy on board ship as you are on land, I think you'd better stay on shore,' Alejandro announced.

If I'd expected my dear brother to jump to my defence, I could have waited forever. I glared at the two boys as we walked along the remainder of the causeway towards the club house, and Donal's Bar.

'I could say the same for you,' I threw back, feeling hotter by the second – and it wasn't all due to the sun. He chose to ignore my remark and started chatting to Kevin.

I glanced surreptitiously at the tall, well-built stranger who was going to be my companion on board the *Golden Goddess* for the next six weeks and decided I hated him.

He was arrogant, egotistical and superior. Who did he think he was, anyway?

Then I answered my own question: the son of your boss – that's who. Inwardly, I groaned. Wasn't it just my luck to fall foul of the one boy on the whole of Mallorca who I'd be stuck with for the duration of what could have been a fantastic holiday? Slowly, the whole idea was beginning to turn sour.

I walked along in silence, watching my traitor brother chatting to *him* as though they were long-lost friends. How could he? I fumed inwardly. After that . . . that *being* had been so nasty?

The soles of my feet were beginning to burn from the hot tarmac under my rubber shoes and a fly persistently attacked my neck. It was quickly joined by a second. I hate flies. In fact, I have always had great sympathy for all animals after seeing how they can be tormented by bluebottles in the countryside. Now, I swotted one as it perched cheekily on my forearm.

I missed it.

I changed my hold-all to my other shoulder and began to wish that I was at home, curled up with a good book. Or watching the telly – anywhere but tramping along in the blazing sun in the middle of nowhere.

'Is it much further?' I directed my question at Kevin, knowing he couldn't possibly know the answer, but refusing to direct any remark to *him*.

'Unfit, are you?' came *his* cool reply, the words loaded with innuendo.

This time, I ignored the remark. Pointedly, I glanced at my Swatch – and nearly made a double-take. 'It's gone two,' I wheezed.

'Three, actually,' *he* said, without looking in my direction.

Not to be outdone, I grabbed Kevin's wrist and checked by his watch.

'Two,' I reiterated.

'Three,' came the bored response.

'Kevin?' I could hear the slight pleading tone in my own voice. 'Your watch is right, isn't it?'

Kevin smiled apologetically at me. 'So's yours, sis, but Alex is right. There's an hour's difference here.'

A lump had formed in my throat but I swallowed it, and managed to remark how stupid it was to mess about with the time.

'Almost as stupid as driving on the right, I suppose?'

I chose to ignore him again.

I felt, rather than saw Kevin glance from Alex to me. I knew he was beginning to get embarrassed by the obvious and unmistakable wall of animosity that had developed between us, but there was no way I was going to give in. As far as I could work out, I was completely blameless. The whole fault lay squarely in *his* corner. First, *he* had almost run me down because he wasn't looking where he was going – second *he* had been unpardonably rude, with no provocation from me. And third, he'd clearly been riding too fast along the causeway and had been unable to stop in time to avoid hitting me – me, a mere pedestrian – which had resulted in his swerving and falling off the moped.

All his fault entirely. And the fact that he persisted in being, well, openly hostile was a polite way of describing his behaviour, only added fuel to the fire.

I drew in a deep, steadying breath, and assumed my most aloof manner. Normally, I got on really well with all of Kevin's friends. Down at the club house, I was treated like one of the boys – something I was proud of. I could never understand some of my girl friends being nervous around boys. They were really just the same as girls – only different – if you see what I mean.

Remembering the great gang we had at the sailing club made me feel a whole lot better. I was being silly, I told myself, to let a stranger annoy me. He was obviously immature and the Spanish half of him, I reasoned, was used to behaving in a macho fashion. I smiled to myself. All I had to do was to treat him as I would any other boy who thought too much of himself and tried to put me down. I'd ignore him. Simply pretend he wasn't there. That way I would avoid verbal fisticuffs and any bad atmosphere. After all, I concluded, I was here to work for six weeks for Rosie and José – I was not working for Alejandro, or Alex, as he asked Kevin to call him.

'You okay, sis?'

I smiled brightly up at Kevin, showing my brother and *him* that I was fine. I was so busy holding my tinsel-bright smile that I didn't see the bollard until I stubbed my toe against it. The pain made me hop about in agony, I was still hopping when I followed the two boys up the stone steps to Donal's Bar.

Rosie, I decided after five minutes, was a zany lady. She had wild red hair, a remarkable suntan and, for a boating lady, amazingly long scarlet nails. Looking back, I guess I should have questioned how she kept them looking so good, but at the time I simply thought how impressive they looked.

José was an older version of his son. Tall, rangy and muscular with a mop of shiny black curls and liquid dark eyes. But, unlike his son, José smiled a lot – showing large white teeth, one of which was capped in gold, giving him an exotic air.

'Finish your drinks, kids, then we'll take you along to the *Goddess* to get acquainted.' Rosie pointed to my bag. 'I hope you've brought some cooler clothes than the ones you've got on, Susan.'

'Oh, I have. Don't worry. But it was freezing cold, and bucketing down when we left London this morning.'

José finished a beer he'd been drinking before laughing good-naturedly. 'It seems odd to you that only two hours flight away, we have such lovely sunshine, no?'

'Too true, sir,' Kevin replied.

José stopped smiling. 'I may be the captain of the *Golden Goddess*, Kevin,' he said, kindly, 'but please, call me José. I do not like the "sir" bit. Roger and Kim are like family to us and we like to think you will treat us the same.'

Kevin lowered his gaze and nodded. 'That's fine by me, José,' he replied.

'And I'm Rosie – to everyone. Now—' she stood up and beckoned to the young girl who had served us our drinks, 'let's take you to the boat, shall we?'

As José paid for our drinks, Alex said, 'You don't need me to go with you, do you?'

I caught a glower cross his father's face.

'Where do you think you are going?' José asked.

Alex breezed along beside us as we walked out of Donal's and started along the quay towards the club house.

'Well, I thought I'd better go up to the villa and change,' Alex replied, adding, 'my present appearance is not very presentable.'

'You can change on the boat,' his father told him, curtly.

'But my clean shorts and shirt are at home.' Alex began to look belligerent.

'Don't argue over such a small point. Not when our guests have just arrived.' Rosie fixed her slanted, green eyes on her husband. 'Let him go and change, for goodness' sake, José. There's no point in his hanging round while we show Susan and Kevin the boat.' She turned and placed a hand on Alex's arm. 'We'll see you at the villa, later,' she told him. 'Oh, and while you're there, get some dog food out of the freezer for Nelson. I forgot this morning.'

'Sure, Mum.' Alex dropped a familiar kiss on his mother's cheek. I couldn't help but notice that as he did, a conspiratorial look was exchanged between mother and son. It didn't need a genius to see that Rosie adored him.

Picking up his moped, he called, 'See you later Kevin,' waved to his parents, then turned and chugged the engine alive.

'Sure,' Kevin called as Alex started to move away.

If the fact that Alex had purposefully snubbed me was noticed, no one let on. Or maybe, I thought as I followed Rosie, Kevin and José along the concrete hard standing which led to the club house, all Spanish men behaved like that.

I suddenly felt very hot and sticky, and tired. But most of all, I was starving. We hadn't eaten since breakfast on the plane – what Kevin aptly called, plastic food – and that was hours ago.

But the moment we stood before the *Golden Goddess*, moored majestically in the still, clear waters of the marina Club de Vela, any desire to eat momentarily disappeared.

'Wow!' Kevin mouthed, in awe. 'She is a beauty.'

José and Rosie looked pleased.

I stared at the gleaming, white-painted hull and solid teak deck, shining expensively in the sunlight. The sails were furled and near the top of the main mast, a very elaborate radar reflector sparkled brilliantly against the azure sky. At the top of the mast, a triangular flag lay limp in the still, warm air, and I noticed the red and yellow Spanish ensign secured at the stern. The thing that impressed me most was the sheer size of the boat. Compared to anything I'd ever sailed, this really *was* like looking at the *Q.E.II*! Suddenly, all my old apprehension and worries came tumbling back. How would I cope with crewing on a boat as big as a mountain?

I glanced across at Kevin. He didn't look at all worried. In fact, he was grinning from ear to ear.

'Leave your luggage there – it will be quite safe – and let's get aboard and show you round.' José indicated for me to climb up the gangplank which led from the quay on to the stern of the *Golden Goddess*.

'Come on, follow me,' Rosie called, walking ahead and crossing the gangplank in a few easy strides. Swallowing a deep breath, I followed. Once on board, I copied Rosie's example and bent to take off my shoes so as not to scuff the beautiful solid teak. Kevin and José followed us quickly shedding their shoes, placing them next to ours on the wooden deck.

'You show Susan below, Rosie, while I take Kevin around up top.' José flashed his gold tooth at me, as he said, 'Do you mind cooking in a galley?'

'No, not at all,' I replied. I liked José with his quick smile and gentle but authoritative voice. 'In fact,' I added, 'I quite enjoy the challenge.'

Rosie grabbed my arm and squeezed it. 'There, I knew you'd be a wonderful help. Kim and Roger have talked so much about you two over the years. I feel I know you like my own daughter.' She began to lead the way along the cockpit towards the main hatchway. Glancing over her tanned shoulder as she walked, she said, 'I have to confess that cooking isn't something I like, Susan.' She gave a short laugh. 'When it is only José, me and the kids, I usually don't bother. Just have lots of tinned stuff in store and the deep freeze stacked with convenience foods.'

I was about to ask Rosie how many children she had – as neither Kim nor Roger had even mentioned Alex – when she stopped and turned to face me.

I back-stepped just in time to avoid bumping into her.

'Do you have a steady boyfriend back in England?' she asked, taking me totally by surprise.

'Er . . . no. Not really,' I admitted, wondering if I were saying the right thing.

A frown puckered her forehead. 'Oh, dear!' She didn't sound very happy.

So I elaborated. 'Well, I haven't exactly *a* boyfriend, as such,' I told her. 'But I do have a whole bunch of boys who are friends, if you see what I mean?'

She nodded – but that piece of news didn't appear to make her any happier.

'Why?' I ventured.

Rosie shrugged. 'Well, Susan, it might have helped if you had.'

I was more puzzled than ever. 'But why?'

She let out a short, sharp sigh, then turned to begin descending the few steps into what turned out to be the main saloon. It was capacious and luxurious with its immaculate cream and gold fittings.

Rosie spread her arms in a wide sweep. 'What do you think of my lovely *Golden Goddess*?' She twirled round like an excited schoolgirl. For a moment, I wondered how old she was. It was difficult to judge.

'It's beautiful,' I told her, more than a bit confused by her sudden change of conversation.

'It is, isn't it? I chose the colour scheme myself, you know?'

'It really is lovely.' I glanced at the sleek, uncluttered interior and gleaming teak and brass fittings. 'You've plenty of handholds, that's for sure,' I observed, wryly.

Rosie picked up a silky red-gold cushion and hugged it to her. It was almost the same colour as her amazing halo of hair.

'Oh, I do love this boat!' she enthused, smiling at me gleefully over the edge of the satin trim. 'José promised to buy it for me if I agreed to marry him. I mean, how could I refuse?'

I raised my eyebrows in surprise. 'That's certainly some wedding present,' I told her.

The cushion was replaced with loving care alongside the pile of others on one of the deep settees which I assumed, like most boats, would probably convert into a double-bed.

Rosie was walking round the saloon towards a teak-lined interior fitment.

'Well, I had to wait long enough for it. When I left show business to marry José, all he owned was a couple of fishing boats.'

'Really?' I was watching as she pressed a small button and a section of the fitment flapped down to reveal a well-stocked drinks cabinet.

'Now he owns a whole fleet,' she continued, as she took out a heavy-bottomed tumbler and a bottle of pink-coloured liquid. She waved the bottle at me. 'Like a drink? It's rather nice. Campari.' As if suddenly taking stock of who she was talking to, she clicked her tongue. 'No, of course you wouldn't like it. It's rather bitter and you're far too young to appreciate it. I'll get you a coke from the galley.'

She poured herself a drink, adding cubes of ice from a silver ice-bucket, before re-pressing the button. The drinks cabinet became a teak fitment again. It was all very impressive, and a million light years away from our small, fibre-glass sailing dinghy back home.

Sipping her pink, iced drink Rosie led me from the main saloon to the fore-cabins.

'Nice, eh?' Rosie said, holding open the heavy door for me to see the bathroom inside.

I nodded. It was like having an inspection of a mini hotel. Five star, at that! You could easily forget you were even on a boat. Except that through every porthole and window I glimpsed the clear, calm amethyst waters of the Mediterranean.

The galley was a little cramped compared to the rest of the cabins, although compact, well-ventilated and lit. It was situated by the main hatchway and it boasted a full stove and oven, small fridge and sink. Tucked at one side under the worktop, was even an upright freezer.

'What luxury!' I enthused, after Rosie had shown me round.

Not in this climate, Susan,' Rosie replied. 'Spain isn't like England, remember. Food goes off very quickly here. Also we're always needing tons of ice for drinks. Talking of which,' she said, 'how about that coke?'

I wanted to say, I'd prefer a sandwich, but accepted

the coke – anything to stop the hunger pangs which were painfully reminding me my tummy wanted something more inside it than sea air.

'How many children do you have?' I asked, politely, as I followed Rosie out of the u-shaped galley and back into the main saloon.

'Two. Didn't you know?' She sank down on to one of the curved, cushioned seats designed to half-circle a teak table.

I swallowed my mouthful of chilled coke, then shook my head.

'I didn't know you had any – until we met Alex.'

As if I'd reminded her of something, she firmly placed her glass on the table, sat back and surveyed me keenly.

I began to feel distinctly uncomfortable under her cool, green gaze.

'So – what do you think of my Alex?' she asked, at length.

What did I think of him? The thought whizzed through my head of telling her he was everything I disliked in a boy. That he was the pits!

What came out was a lame, 'Oh, he's – er, nice.'

The green gaze didn't falter for a second. Then Rosie shook her auburn curls off her narrow, cinnamon-brown shoulders and rolled her eyes to the cabin ceiling.

'He's not,' she said, flatly.

'Pardon?'

The emerald eyes came back to settle on me. 'Nice,' she told me. 'Alex is *not* nice.'

'Oh?' What else could I say?

'He's anything but, I'm afraid.' She let out a deep, exasperated sigh, then narrowed her gaze at me. 'Look, Susan, I like you, so I want to warn you. Sort of woman to woman, you understand?' I nodded, perplexed, as she continued. 'The truth is, although he's my son, and I love him a lot, I don't actually like him very much. At least,' she quickly went on to explain, 'not when it comes to the way he treats girls.' She paused, and studied me closer.

'You do understand what I'm getting at, don't you?'

I didn't, but I said that I thought I did.

She patted the settee and obediently, I walked round to sit beside her.

Leaning closer she lowered her voice to whisper 'He's terrible with girls!'

'He is?' I hoped my voice sounded suitably concerned.

The red curls bounced as Rosie confirmed her own statement. 'Terrible!' It was almost an anguished sigh. 'Really,' her voice was even lower. 'I don't know where he gets it from. His father was never a playboy. Once he saw me dancing at Tito's nightclub, that was it. There was never ever another woman for him. And he was the only man for me. Poor Roger was heartbroken, you know? He thought I would eventually marry him.' She gave a quick, bright smile. 'But Kim came along to mend his broken heart. I was so glad.' She sighed, as if remembering. 'Dear José, to think when I agreed to give up treading the boards to marry him, I would be marrying a man who'd become almost a self-made millionaire.'

29

Now I *was* impressed. I was intrigued, as well. About Alex. I wanted to know more.

'How do you mean, about Alex – and girls?' I ventured.

Rosie jumped, startled out of her reverie.

'How? Why, how else? He's the original playboy, that's how. Do you know, Susan, I haven't met one girl who hasn't fallen for my Alex the moment she met him?'

'Well, you have now!' I all but burst out. Then glanced across at Rosie, worried, in case the grittiness of my tone might have offended her.

But she was smiling, a sort of knowing smile.

'No, it's true,' I assured her. Then added, sitting up straight to bring home my point more seriously and, hopefully, believably, 'I'm afraid he and I didn't hit it off from the start. If anything, to be truthful, we really don't like each other, *at all*,' I ended, for good measure.

Rosie shook her head, smiling indulgently at me.

'Oh dear, Susan. So he's already worked some of the old Alex magic on you, eh?'

'What?' I retorted, once more confused by Rosie's grasshopper conversation.

'It's all part of the act, my dear. Don't you see? And you've fallen for it. He starts off by being really obnoxious. Gets a girl's adrenalin going. That's step one. Next, he turns on the Latin charm – and that gets the girl's emotions going. Step two. Once he's won them over – it's like watching a re-run of an old movie, I'm afraid.'

'What is?' I was beginning to react like a cornered

cat and I was ready to pounce, with all my claws out.

'Step three, of course, he drops them. Wham! Right on their pretty butts.' She finished the last of her Campari, placed the empty glass firmly on the shiny table top, then stood up. 'So be warned. Now come on,' she said, 'let's join the men aloft.'

Silently, I started to follow her up on to the deck. To make conversation I asked Rosie about her second child. She laughed happily.

'Oh, you'll like Pilar,' she replied. 'She's open and straight. Quite lovely. There's no devious corners to my little girl. She's in Marbella at the moment with friends,' she continued, 'but she'll be back in a few days, before the first charter family arrives.'

'How old is she?' I enquired, thinking for some reason that she was probably much younger than Alex.

To my surprise, Rosie told me Pilar was Alex's twin.

She slipped an arm companionably round my waist as we made our way out into glorious sunlight, to the cockpit where José and Kevin were lazing on the spacious deck.

'You won't tell Alex what I've said, will you?' Rosie whispered 'Keep it as our secret. I just don't want you going back to England with a broken heart as well as a suntan.'

I managed a quick, bright smile. 'Don't worry, Rosie,' I said. 'I've no intention of *that* happening, either.' And certainly not with someone as awful as Alex, I was going to add. But didn't, of course. There was no need to be personal. He wasn't worth it.

Chapter 3

'Do you want a quick tour of the upper decks, Susan?' José asked as Rosie and I joined him. 'Or will you wait until tomorrow? I've a feeling we should be offering you something to eat. You must be hungry?'

It was a close contest, but my stomach won over my curiosity about the anatomy of the boat.

'You'll have to get used to our Spanish ways, I think,' José was saying as we walked back along the quay, a few minutes later. 'In my country, we do not eat our lunch until after two – usually not until three.'

'Three!' I stared wide-eyed at him, which made him laugh loudly and clap a firm, large hand on my shoulder.

'It is very hot here. We have a different timetable to you people from the northern climates. We make an early start, when the sun isn't too hot. We finish work, then have our midday meal – except it is, as I say, about three. Then we siesta, when the sun is fierce and wake up to enjoy the remainder of the afternoon and cool evening.'

'Sounds fine by me,' Kevin chirped up.

We picked up our bags where we'd dumped them

then walked through the grounds of the club house. José had a few words with one of the stewards then the automatic doors were opened, and we walked through to a private car parking area.

'Our villa is up in the mountains. Not too far. We can see the harbour and the boats from the terrace,' Rosie told us as José opened the doors of a massive white Mercedes.

Kevin and I placed our luggage in the boot, then piled into the back of the sumptuous car. As we shut the doors, I went to wind down a window but Rosie stopped me.

'The air-conditioning will come on in a second,' she told me. 'It's cooler than opening the windows and does less damage to your hairstyle.' She glanced back at me, then laughed. 'Mind you, with your wonderful thick hair, I doubt you have any problems with looking good all the time.'

'Susan? Good-looking?' Kevin bantered, grabbing my ponytail and tugging it playfully. 'She's far too much of a tomboy to ever be that.'

'That's because you're her brother,' Rosie replied, her expression serious. 'You'd be surprised how the local lads will fall for Susan's cool, blonde looks.'

I began to feel embarrassed. They were discussing me as if I wasn't there. To change the subject, I asked when the first people were going to arrive to charter the *Golden Goddess*.

'Saturday,' José replied, over his shoulder as he manoeuvred the large, smooth-running car on to a narrow road and began driving west, heading towards the distant pine-covered hills.

'Pilar is due back Thursday or Friday,' Rosie announced. She hitched her long legs under her and turned to talk to Kevin. 'You'll like Pilar. She's great fun.'

Kevin looked perplexed. 'Who's she?'

'Alex's twin sister,' I informed him, realizing nothing had been mentioned to him about her before.

'She's going to study languages after the holidays in the south of England. Brighton. Is that far from your house?'

'Yes!' 'No!' both Kevin and I said in unison.

I turned to him. 'It is far, Kevin,' I insisted.

'Depends,' Kevin argued.

Rosie looked amused. A tiny smile tugged at her glossed lips. 'Depends on what?' she asked.

'On what you're driving, and who you're going to meet,' Kevin told her, matching her smile with a cheeky one of his own.

José, who'd been listening to the conversation, gave a throaty chuckle.

'You've a good point there, Kevin. But watch out for Pilar. She's a lovely young lady, but she is like her brother – *escorpión*.'

'Sorry, I don't understand?' Kevin frowned, then clicked his fingers. 'Ah. You mean she is, a scorpion? As with a sting in its tail?'

'That is correct – exactly.' José nodded at us through the driving mirror. 'A sting in her tail.'

'I'll bear that in mind,' Kevin told him, then fell into a general conversation about the boat – and the possible passages planned for the *Golden Goddess*.

I listened with half an ear, but mainly my attention

strayed to the surrounding countryside as we covered the distance at an easy speed. The only thing that worried me as we rounded blind bends in the mountain road, was the chance of meeting something coming in the opposite direction. Luckily, there didn't seem to be much traffic. Rosie said most people were either at the beaches, on their boats, or preparing lunch at home.

'Or in the restaurants,' José added. 'Did you kids know there are more restaurants in Mallorca than any other Mediterranean island? For every one that closes, two open!'

He hooted the car horn loudly as we approached yet another hairpin bend. One side was jagged rock – the other, a sheer drop down the mountainside, to the road below. I tried not to think about it.

Then, just as we rounded the corner, a moped flashed into view in the centre of the road. There was a second's hesitation, then the moped swerved dangerously and skirted the wrong side of the car, before disappearing round the bend. But in that instant, I caught a glimpse of familiar, thick, black curls and a pair of long, suntanned legs. The surprised dark eyes were familiar, too.

'That crazy idiot!' José exploded, in fury. 'He drives like a maniac. And where does he think he is going?'

Rosie patted her husband's muscular forearm and tried to calm him. But José continued to look really angry. He was still seething as we entered the shrub-lined drive to their villa.

'I thought he had come back to change?' José

stormed, as the car screeched to a halt, accompanied by a spray of gravel from under all four wheels.

'Don't be so Spanish, darling,' Rosie chided him gently.

We opened the doors and piled out in front of a long, ranch-type, whitewashed villa.

Jose's scowl began to disappear as he saw Rosie smiling at him.

'There, that's better,' she pandered to him. 'You mustn't lose your temper when we've guests.'

José's gold tooth gleamed as he smiled apologetically. 'You're right, Rosie. Besides, it sends my blood pressure up, and that's *loco*. Now, kids,' he turned his attention to me, 'grab your bags and let's go see what Marie-Carmen has prepared as a welcome lunch.'

Kevin let out a low whistle as we walked, side by side, up to the front of the film-set styled villa. It was built on a slight incline, surrounded on all sides by flowering trees and shrubs – a riot of deep pinks, apricots and brilliant white. Huge scarlet heads of geraniums splashed their brilliance against the white background of the walls, while tall, dark-green pine trees and lighter, silvery green eucalyptuses swayed majestically in the light breeze wafting up from the sea, far below.

The view of the bay and the club house was spectacular. The boats in the marina appeared like a gaggle of white geese bobbing on the cobalt-blue water. Sunlight sparkled and danced off the small waves like a million diamonds, and the air was heavy with the scent of flowers and pines. Apart from our feet crunching over the gravel and a dog barking somewhere from behind the house, all that we could hear were the notes of the birds and now and then the mounting crescendo of cicadas. Not that I knew they were cicadas until know-all Kev told me.

'Are you sure that tremendous noise is from those tiny little creatures?' I queried, hardly believing it.

'Too true,' came the reply. 'Sounds like a million electric cables sizzling with energy, doesn't it?'

'Weird!' I announced, then hurried to catch up with the others as they entered the villa through the massive, studded oak door.

'Until we're ready to sail, I've given you adjoining rooms at the back of the villa,' Rosie announced as she led us through the wide, cool hall and along a narrow passageway – one of many which led off the central, square hall.

We passed interesting paintings, vivid with applied oils, mostly depicting what I assumed were views of the island. Here and there, huge earthenware Aladdin-type pots, overhanging with ferns and creepers, adorned the interior.

Rosie stopped and threw open one of the doors off the passageway. Kevin and I followed her silently into the bedroom. It was lavishly furnished with a double-bed, matching carved dark oak bedside tables, a wall-to-wall row of wardrobes and a small, round table draped with a floor-length tablecloth in old lace.

'This will be yours, Kevin,' Rosie announced as

she began to walk through the room towards a door at the far end. 'And this will be for you, Susan,' she said.

The adjoining room was almost identical, with the same exposed pine beams running across the ceiling. But the bedhead, side tables and matching dressing-table were of a light-coloured, basket-weave bamboo. The bedcover, and curtains which fluttered slightly in the warm, scented breeze were of a muted pink, green and lavender design. The floor, like all the others in the villa, was pale cream ceramic tiles. Against the whitewashed walls, the few carefully selected paintings stood out starkly. I decided, in an absent-minded sort of way that they were very good.

'Like it?' Rosie was observing me, a twinkle of delight in her green eyes.

I sighed happily. 'It's beaut!'

'Great. Okay kids, I'd suggest you freshen up then make your way out to the back. Lunch will be waiting.' She stopped as she reached a door that was at the opposite end of the room to the one we'd entered. 'By the way, there's a bathroom across the passageway and this door, Susan, leads out into the same passage. If there's anything you need, yell!'

I nodded. Then called after her, 'What shall I wear for lunch, Rosie?'

She stopped in the doorway. 'Something casual. Wear your bathing costume too, if you like. If you fancy the idea, you could have a dip in the pool before eating.' As she closed the door after her I ran and threw myself on the wide bed.

'So, what do you think of it so far?' I asked Kevin, out of habit.

As usual, Kev answered. 'Not a lot.'

I sat up straight. 'Are you joking?'

He pulled a face, as he walked to his room. 'I'm joking!'

I giggled, lay back on my bed and kicked off my shoes. 'What do you think of José and Rosie?'

'They're okay,' Kevin said. 'Alex isn't a bad sort, once you get to know him.'

'Forget it!' I rolled over and rested my chin in my hands.

'Forget what?' Kevin stopped as he reached his door.

'*Him*. You know – Don Juan.'

'Hey, kiddo, whatever makes you call him that? He hasn't been stupid enough to make a pass at you, has he?'

I snorted. 'Just let him try, that's all.'

Kevin started to laugh, softly.

'Oh, and just what's so funny?' I don't like being laughed at – especially when I don't know what the joke is.

'*You* are, kid. I mean, what makes you think a skinny, pale-faced baby like you could ever attract a bloke like Alex? He's way out of your league.'

Furious, I grabbed my nearest shoe, then aimed it at Kevin's smug face. 'Get out!' I hissed.

My shoe missed by miles, but the message got home. Kevin ducked, ran into his room and shut the door between us.

I rolled off the bed, walked over to where I'd

dumped my hold-all on the floor, unzipped it, then began to take out the few clothes I'd brought with me. Apart from the things I'd travelled in, I'd brought two pairs of cotton trousers, three pairs of shorts, a collection of T-shirts, underwear, and three bathing costumes. Well, actually, there were two one-pieces and a pretty skimpy bikini. I arranged the clothes on hangers in the wardrobe and in the drawers, then pondered as to what I should put on. Casual, Rosie had said. Well, I guessed a pair of shorts and T-shirt would be casual enough.

I settled for my bright yellow shorts and matching, spotted halter top. Underneath, I had on my yellow and black cossie. But first, I decided, suddenly feeling very hot, sticky and a mess, I needed a shower.

Kevin grunted as I popped my head round his door to tell him I was going to the bathroom.

'I think I'll have one, too,' he called after me. 'So, don't be long.'

'I'll be like lightning, don't worry.'

The bathroom was decorated in a similar fashion to the rest of the house, except the ceramic tiles also covered the walls. A contrast was made with varying shades of green. Green ferns cascaded down the wall nearest the opaque window, a pile of different sized towels, ranging from the deepest bottle-green to the palest olive, was arranged attractively on display shelves, while several bottles of bath preparations, in crystal bottles, lined the deep bath area.

Apart from the tub, twin washbasins, toilet and bidet, there was a large walk-in shower, shielded by a pretty, lacy curtain.

Just like a film-set, I thought, as I turned on the mixer tape and waited for the water to get to the right temperature. Then I piled my hair into a plastic cap I'd discovered, and stepped gingerly under the jet of cool water.

It was bliss. Wonderful! I almost felt the water washing away the grit and grime, and tiredness from my body. After a few minutes, I grabbed my flannel and a bar of soap and began to wash my face and neck, arms and tummy – luxuriating in the sensation of the running water.

When I'd finished, I stood still to let the water cascade over me. It trickled in a steady stream over my head, down my face and between my small breasts. A puddle had collected in the basin at my feet and happily I splashed around in it.

I was just thinking about turning off the shower when I heard someone walk in. I assumed it was Kevin and opened my mouth to tell him to wait. What happened was that I got a mouthful of warm water!

'Pass me a towel, will you?' I called, pushing my arm round the shower curtain.

'Sure, anything to oblige,' came the amused reply. Only it wasn't Kevin. It was Alex.

I blushed – then panicked. The first thing I did was make a grab for the curtain and wrapped it round me. Then, furious, I peered out.

As if it were the most natural thing in the world, Alex brazenly handed me a towel.

'If it wasn't for the plastic hat, you could almost pass for a mermaid.' He grinned, and his eyes began

to lazily wander over my face, my neck, my shoulders
. . . as I frantically tried to hitch up the flimsy shower
curtain to cover as much of me as I could.

'Do you usually walk into bathrooms, unannounced?' I flared.

Amusement lit Alex's eyes. 'We're very relaxed in
this house,' came his reply. 'That's why we don't
have locks on bathroom doors.'

'Well, just unrelax and get out!' Angrily, I pulled
the cap off my head. My loosened hair tumbled over
my shoulders. I grabbed the towel he still proferred
and pointed with my other hand for him to quit the
room. But as that was the hand that was holding the
curtain, I suddenly found I was standing half-naked
before I'd pulled the towel against me.

'Don't get so worried,' Alex said, backing towards
the door, open amusement now tugging at his mouth.
'I like my girls with more curves – or should I say,
with at least some curves.'

I'd just got hold of the soap to throw at him when
the door closed, leaving me fuming and hotter than
I'd been when I'd first got under the shower.

'He's a pig!' I told the bathmat as I trod on it.

I still thought he was a pig half an hour later when
Kevin and I walked out on to the back patio to join
José and Rosie, and a group of strangers who were
all seated round a long trestle table picturesquely
placed beneath a canopy of pale green vines.

Chapter 4

Whether it was because I was starving, or what, I don't know but the paella Marie-Carmen produced tasted fantastic. The huge, two-handled paella pan was brought to the small table adjacent to the main one and displayed with great ceremony. It was so pretty with its saffron-coloured rice, pink prawns, golden pieces of chicken, black shiny mussel shells and vivid green beans and red peppers that it almost seemed a shame to disturb it.

When Rosie asked if it was the first time we'd tried the Spanish national dish, I'd grinned sheepishly.

'We've had something that calls itself paella,' I'd admitted, 'but it comes pre-cooked and frozen and doesn't taste anything like this.'

'Then you must have some more,' Alex announced, taking my plate and handing it to his mother. He turned to me, his back was to the rest of the guests – mostly it seemed, boating people, too – so they couldn't hear what he was saying.

'We must feed you up while you are with us, Susan. We Spaniards like our women with more curves than the Englishman.'

I blushed furiously, knowing to just what he was referring. But I refused to be drawn into a confrontation. I remembered Rosie's warning about Alex's three steps with girls. Step one was to get them angry.

Well, there is no way you're going to set me up, mister, I decided, devastatingly good-looking though you may be. The trouble is, you know it!

'There, I've embarrassed you,' Alex said. Dark, sardonic brows arched meaningfully at me.

For a split second I had the uncontrollable urge to tip the remains of my rice over his head but I reminded myself at the last minute of what Rosie had told me. With a great effort I forced myself to smile, even though it hurt.

'I like myself as I am,' I told him, evenly. Then purposefully turned my back on him to talk to Kevin. Only Kevin was deep in a boating conversation with the woman next to him so I started to push the rice round on my plate – anything to avoid looking at Alex's smug face again.

'I do hope I haven't put you off your food?' Alex enquired, sounding almost genuinely worried.

I swallowed the desire to tell him to mind his own business, and said, 'I expect you put most girls off their food for one reason or another, Alex.' I hoped my innuendo wasn't totally lost on him.

But his next words showed his ego was intact!

'Yes, I do have that effect on girls, I'm afraid. I think it's my magnetic charm that does it.' He began to reach for the earthenware jug of wine, then stopped and reached for the bottle of lemonade instead. 'I keep forgetting you're too young for wine,' he said, deprecatingly. 'Although here in Spain, being a more civilized country we are introduced to wine with our food when we are very young. We grow to respect it, not get drunk on it.'

I wondered what he'd look like with the earthenware jug sitting on his ears!

'Alex?' Rosie's voice carried the length of the table. There was an unmistakable edge to it. 'Are you seeing that our guests are well looked after down that end?'

Alex gave his mother one of his disarming smiles. 'Of course,' he assured her, then turned his smile on me. It didn't seem to have the effect he'd expected. 'You are enjoying yourself, aren't you, Susan?'

I couldn't quite work out if he was being sarcastic, or genuine. I opted for the sarcasm. After all, he'd seemed to do nothing else since we'd first met but be rude and objectionable. The thought flashed through my mind that maybe Spanish girls liked that sort of behaviour. But I threw the idea out fast. I wasn't Spanish, and I didn't like him!

'Would it be awfully impolite,' I asked softly, with my very best English accent, 'if I told you I'd be overjoyed if you weren't around?'

A moment's confusion — and then anger flared in his dark eyes. He stood up, scraping back the chair he'd been sitting on. Their dog — a beautiful boxer with yellow eyes who'd been lying at Alex's side — jumped up in fright. If looks could have killed, Alex's glare would have put me under the table.

'As I said before,' he directed at me as he passed by, 'you are very childish.' Then he stalked down the length of the table, to disappear inside the villa.

I glanced up, red-cheeked and a bit ashamed of my behaviour to find Kevin studying me.

'You okay, sis?' he asked, quietly.

I nodded, not daring to speak. For some silly reason I felt a constriction in my throat and tears began to well in my eyes. I played with the fork on my plate, willing the tears to go away, but a great wave of self-pity swept over me. Drawing in a deep, steadying breath I tried to work out what was happening? Why was this dream holiday turning into a nightmare? The answer was simple. *HIM!*

And then the terrifying thought whizzed into my head: He's done it! Alex has managed to get your emotions in a tizzy. The adrenalin flowing. Step one!

Don't be daft, my saner self interrupted. He's had the opposite effect. Sure you're all churned up over him, but not because you fancy him – far from it.

I had just decided I was over-reacting because I was tired and a bit homesick and maybe just a bit nervous, when there was a great deal of clapping and chatter at the far end of the table.

I glanced up, not knowing what I expected to see. What I saw was Alex carefully carrying a huge, elaborately decorated gateau.

'There, everyone. Isn't that a pretty sight?' Rosie had got to her feet and was accompanying Alex – plus cake – towards us.

I leaned to one side and Kevin leaned to the other to make room as Alex placed the cake on the table in front of us.

'Hey, see the message?' the woman to Kevin's left

exclaimed. 'Isn't that nice? *Welcome to Kevin and Susan – Happy Sailing!*'

I glanced up at Rosie and smiled. 'You shouldn't have—' I began, overwhelmed at such a kind gesture, but Rosie was shaking her head.

'Not me – Alex,' she cut in. 'It was all my dear son's idea. Just shows you, doesn't it?' She turned and hugged Alex. 'You're not all bad, are you, darling? You even surprise me sometimes, and I'm your mother!' Rosie lent over and hooked her arm through Alex's, then gave him a quick, motherly kiss on his angular, bronzed cheek.

José, who'd been listening with a surprised expression on his craggy face, raised the half-filled wine goblet to his son. 'Well, here's to you,' he said, a note of pride in his voice. He smiled round at the rest of his guests. 'And to think I was under the impression that all my young son ever thought about was girls. And more girls,' he added, laughing.

'Alex is full of contradictions,' Rosie remarked, proudly.

I suddenly felt very small and petty, and insignificant. There was no way I could bring myself to meet Alex's eye. Luckily, I didn't have to as Kevin thanked him for us.

When I'd finally plucked up courage to look in his direction he had his back to me, and was busy talking to the Englishwoman who, it seemed, also had a boat in the harbour.

Bright sunlight and bird song woke me the following morning. I stretched lazily, becoming vaguely aware of a tightness on my shoulders where I'd managed to get a slight tan. I relaxed for a few more minutes, mentally going over the events of the previous afternoon. After lunch Kevin and Alex had decided to play tennis at a place called the La Mola club, on the far side of the bay. When Alex had asked if I'd like to join them, I'd quickly declined his offer. Not that I don't like tennis – I do. But I'm choosey about who I play with. I think he got the message.

Rosie had insisted she showed me over the villa, and the garden.

'I prefer the jacuzzi,' Rosie had told me as we stood at the deep end of an impressive pool. The water had looked so cool and inviting I wanted to dive straight in.

'I take it you can swim?' Rosie had said.

I'd nodded. 'I've my advanced life-saving certificate.'

'Makes sense. I suppose it's one of the requisites for teaching at the sailing school?'

'A priority,' I'd assured her.

Rosie had trailed a long crimson nail through the water, then giggled. 'I'm pretty formidable on a Lilo,' she'd joked. 'But if you ever see me floundering in deep water just throw me a life-jacket. Don't forget.'

I'd promised her I'd make a note across the life raft on the *Goddess*.

She'd left me then, to go in for her siesta.

'Sure you'll be okay?' she'd called over her shoulder as she'd mounted the terrace steps.

'Of course,' I'd replied, then turned and made a racing dive into the aquamarine water.

I'd mucked about in the pool for about an hour, then gone back into the villa, out of the glaring sun. I'd showered and lain down for a while, then must have fallen asleep. When I'd woken it had been nearly seven. I'd joined the others on the terrace, feeling a bit embarrassed and still tired. After dinner, I'd excused myself and headed back to bed.

Now, I slipped from under the sheet and ran over to the sliding doors which led on to a balcony. The view in the early morning light was breathtakingly beautiful. To one side, were the mountains – mist-covered with the morning heat. To the left I caught sight of the turquoise sea with the muted colours of the old houses lining the natural harbour. The air was perfectly still. There was no traffic. Even the birds seemed hushed in the tranquillity of the moment. I glanced around. The house appeared to be isolated in a large amount of ground. The only other houses I could see were a long way off, just the white of flat roofs, or sections of plastered walls showing between the sentinel pines.

Below, the dark-green, spiky grass glistened with early morning dew. The abundant array of strange, exotic-looking flowering shrubs and plants seemed almost too bright to be real in the shimmering light. The slight haze on the mountains and hanging over the distant sea indicated the heat to come. As it was, it must have been up in the seventies, I decided, because although I wore only a thin cotton sleep shirt, I felt warm.

I let my gaze wander back to the sea. I couldn't

wait to get down there. It had to be heaven, I thought, to sail on a sea so calm and clear.

I drew in a final mouthful of flower-scented air, then ran back into my room, grabbed my robe and toilet bag and made for the bathroom.

This time, I made sure the door was jammed by the bathstool. Just remembering about Alex standing there the day before made me grow hot and angry. As for his behaviour over lunch. . . . Then I remembered mine, and could have kicked myself for being so silly! Never mind, I consoled myself as I splashed cold water over my face, that was yesterday. Hopefully, today he'll have vanished off the face of the earth!

Kevin was up and dressed when I knocked on his door, a little later.

'You're looking good, kiddo,' he announced as I flopped on his big double-bed. 'You've got a slight tan already.'

I secured my hair in its elastic band, then turned to face him.

'You don't look too bad yourself. Except your nose is a bit red.'

He bent to examine his face in the wardrobe mirror, then walked across to join me on the bed.

'I got a bit singed on the tennis court. The top of my legs are tender, too.'

I glanced at where his shorts met his thighs. The skin was glowing.

'Better smother yourself with the cream Mum packed,' I advised.

'I did. But I guess I was out in the sun too long for the first day.' He stood up and stretched, then glanced at his watch. 'Come on,' he said, 'we'd better go and see what's happening.'

Walking along the quiet passageway, I enquired as to who'd won the match.

Kevin shrugged. 'Guess.'

'*He* did,' I said, my voice curt and flat.

Kevin eyed me, curiously. 'He does have a name, remember?'

I nodded. 'I remember,' I didn't sound enthusiastic.

The frown on Kevin's forehead deepened. 'Hey, what's up? You usually get on well with my mates. What's the problem?'

I gave a slight shrug. 'I don't know. He just bugs me, that's all.'

Kevin stopped, so I stopped, too.

'He likes you, you know?'

'Oh yeh?' I wasn't about to be convinced.

'Yes. He told me so. He also said he was sorry he'd busted in on you like that in the bathroom. He hadn't realized anyone was in there.'

I stared at Kevin for a full minute, then started to chew on my bottom lip. Finally, I turned and continued to walk along to the hall, heading for the kitchen where I could hear someone moving about.

'Sue, wait, will you?'

I didn't. I kept walking. How could Kevin be so blind? I fumed silently to myself. Couldn't he see Alex was whitewashing himself to look good in his eyes?

Kevin caught me up and placed a hand on my shoulder. 'Don't be like that,' he said.

'Like what?'

He removed his hand. 'Like making problems before the holiday's even begun,' he stated, pointedly. 'You're so pig-headed!'

I stopped short and turned on my brother. 'Look, Kevin, let's get one thing straight, shall we?' I steamed. 'You can believe what you like, and like who you like. But don't ask me to like that ... that. . . .' I stammered to a halt, trying to find a word nasty enough to describe Alex Covas. Finally, and in frustration, I said, '*Him*! Okay?'

Kevin's serious expression suddenly dissolved. 'You know, I do believe, in a peculiar sort of way, you're attracted to him. Falling in love at last, are you?'

I shut my mouth, steeling my gaze. Then asked. 'Are there sharks in the Mediterranean?'

My question surprised him. 'No. Yes. I mean, I think so ... though I'm not too sure if they're man-eaters.'

'Well, never mind. I'll take a chance. Just remember,' I said, turning and walking away from him again, 'if I ever give you the slightest indication that I have any other feelings for *him* apart from a deep, constant loathing, throw me to the nearest shark, okay?'

Kevin burst out laughing. 'Sis, you're over the top!' Then, when he saw I wasn't laughing, he sobered up. 'You're reading him all wrong, kid,' he told me. 'Don't say I didn't warn you.'

Breakfast was served on the patio. Huge, sweet, iced buns which Marie-Carmen called *ensaimadas*, accompanied by strong, milky coffee served in large cups.

I'd just bitten into my second bun, when José and Rosie appeared.

'How did you both sleep?' Rosie enquired, looking vibrant and pretty in a pair of emerald shorts and matching top.

'Great, thanks,' Kevin replied. I nodded in agreement.

Marie-Carmen came hurrying out with fresh coffee and more *ensaimadas* and placed them on the table. She had a rapid conversation in Spanish with Rosie, then bustled away again.

'Marie-Carmen's going into Palma to buy some of the provisions for the boat,' Rosie told us.

'Who's driving her?' José asked, adding, 'Alex?'

Rosie nodded as she flicked a flake of thin pastry off her chin. 'Good,' José sounded relieved, 'That leaves me free to take Kevin and Susan for a sail to get the feel of the boat.' He smiled at us. 'Like the idea?'

'You bet!' I enthused.

Rosie pushed her curls off her face. 'Count me out this morning, darling. I've an appointment at the *peluqueria*'s.'

'But you only had your hair done yesterday.' José looked resigned as he added, 'Women! Between my wife and my daughter, my fortune is spent at the beauty parlour!'

'Nonsense! You know you Spanish men like your women looking well-groomed.'

I watched Rosie's perfectly manicured fingers reach

for the coffee pot, and hid my hands under my thighs. It's not that I bite my nails any more, it's just that they don't seem to grow very long before breaking. Anyway, I reasoned, a girl can't have long nails if she's sailing, can she? Not unless you had a boat like the *Goddess* – where everything was done for you. From what I'd seen the boat was crammed with every latest professional gadget on the market.

I glanced across at Rosie, thinking how feminine and lovely she looked so early in the morning – then found myself wondering what Pilar looked like? If she was anything like her mother, she'd be beautiful. The idea deflated me. I may be many things, but beautiful? Never! I was too angular and lanky. Not, I reminded myself, that I needed nerds like Alex to tell me!

'Okay crew,' José announced, placing his empty cup on the saucer. 'Ready when you are.'

I jumped up, excited by the idea that we were finally going for a sail. José shook his head at me.

'I think you like the sea as much as I do,' he observed. 'Are you a good sailor?'

'She's one of the best!' Kevin replied before I could open my mouth.

José studied me for a second longer then, standing up, he slipped an arm round my shoulders. 'Well, we shall see how you fare on my little lady, shall we? It's a bit bigger than the boats you're used to, I know. But once you have the knowledge of sailing in a small boat, you will be at home in any size vessel. The principles are the same.'

I gulped. I only wished I felt as confident about

the whole venture as he was about us. Still, I wasn't going to say anything to change his opinion. I was too keyed up about sailing on the *Golden Goddess*. In fact, I couldn't wait.

Chapter 5

'Like to take over the helm?' José asked Kevin.

We were sailing back toward Andraitx, having run the *Golden Goddess* along the coast to a place called San Telmo.

'Do you trust me?' Kevin replied, picking his way carefully along the deck from midships, where he'd been checking the mainsail.

'You know how a tiller works, don't you?'

Kevin nodded. 'Sure. But I haven't had much experience on a ship this size.'

'Then it is time you did,' José announced, as Kevin dropped down to join us in the cockpit. 'Just remember, she drives like a car – turn the wheel the way you want the ship to turn. It's simple.'

Kevin wiped the perspiration off his damp forehead. 'It sure makes more sense than having to turn the tiller the opposite direction to the way you want to travel,' he remarked. He hesitated for a moment as José went to pass the wheel over to him. 'You positive about this?' he queried.

'Of course,' came the firm reply. 'Remember, she's not a racer. Just treat her with respect. You'll be all right.'

I glanced up at the sails. The boat was reaching: the wind filling the sails at a ninety-degree angle. It was one of the easiest points of sailing and one Dad had taught us from the very first.

'Want to go about? Get the feel of her?' José asked, after a while.

Kevin looked like a cat with a whole bucket of cream. 'Fine by me, skipper.'

'She's all yours, take her about when you're ready.' José walked over to join me. As he sat down, his eyes skimmed the mast, up to where the flag was fluttering freely in the wind.

'Aye, aye, captain,' Kevin called and made a mock salute, his fingertips skimming the hard lip of his bright scarlet cap. Then he also looked at the flag and tell-tales, checking the direction of the wind before shouting, 'Ready about!' This was quickly followed by, 'Lee-oh!' as he began to bring the *Golden Goddess* through the eye of the wind and skilfully steered the ship on a broad reach.

I watched, fascinated, as the great front genoa and mainsail began to slacken, before the wind began to gust from the opposite side, filling the heavy sail, billowing it out majestically. It was quite a sight!

Without realizing it, as we'd gone about, force of habit had made me duck to avoid the cross movement of the boom. Now, José teased me about it.

'No need to duck on a ship this size, eh Susan?', he said.

I grinned sheepishly. 'Reckon not, skipper. Just give me time to get used to it.'

He'd smiled indulgently. 'You'll soon get accustomed to the *Goddess*, don't worry. Now, you trim the mainsail, I'll tackle the genoa – that baby is too heavy for a little thing like you.'

I didn't need telling twice. On board, you take an order first time round, there may not be time for a second request.

With the sails trimmed, I could feel the *Goddess* pulling ahead on our new tack, out into the open sea.

José clapped his hand on Kevin's shoulder, then put his other hand on mine. 'You make a formidable team,' he told us. 'Bravo!'

Kevin looked pleased. 'She's so easy to handle,' he said. 'I'm surprised.'

'Normally, yes. But like all ships, beware of bad weather.'

'You have bad weather here? It hardly seems possible,' I said, glancing round at the clear cobalt water which looked more like a tranquil duck pond than a sea.

José studied me for a moment, then nodded. 'Maybe not as bad as your Atlantic, but the danger here is sudden squalls. One moment you can be moored and over the side swimming – the next caught in an inland storm. And that's dangerous.' He let out a rueful sigh. 'I nearly lost a boat because I foolishly thought I knew more than Mother Nature. And I'm an old sea horse.'

He must have caught my worried expression

because he laughed suddenly and said, 'Don't concern yourself, Susan, normally we have the problem of intense heat and windless days. That's where my beautiful twin engines come in. But never forget about the sudden strong winds that can blow up without warning in the Med. If it happens when the boat is anchored in a cove, you don't sit about asking questions. You up anchor and get out – quick. Okay?'

'Right!' I said. Then asked, 'Anyone like the galley-hand to fetch them a drink?'

'Now you're talking,' José smiled. 'Make mine a San Miguel.'

'Same for me, sis.'

I ran down to the galley and took two bottles of beer from the fridge, then opened a can of lemonade for myself.

By the time I was aloft again, José was back at the helm.

We sailed in companionable silence for a while, then José glanced up at the sun. It was high over our heads.

'I think we'll run back to port,' he informed us. 'By the time we dock, it will be after two.'

We were about a quarter of a mile off shore when José turned the *Golden Goddess* into the wind in order to drop the sails. Kevin busied himself with roller-reefing the genoa while I secured the mainsail on to the boom. I'd just fastened the last retainer when I noticed a bright blue speedboat bearing down on us – on what looked like a collision course.

'Skipper!' I called, keeping the panic out of my voice. 'There's a boat coming up fast on our starboard side.' Then looking back across the water, I added, 'There's a water skier behind it. No, make that two water skiers on one mono-ski.'

José cut the engines, then put the *Goddess* into reverse. The ship began to move slowly but steadily astern, making as much space as possible between us and the wide sweep the water skiers would cover as the speedboat swung away from us.

'Tontos!' José stormed, his face tight with anger. 'They are pirates, these speedboat owners. They have no right to be allowed out—' His words faded on the wind as the water skiers swept almost under the stern of the Goddess, and the boy and girl waved frantically to us. The next second, they'd let go the guidelines and had simultaneously tumbled into the water.

The engines of the *Goddess* suddenly cut out and José ordered Kevin to drop the Jacob's ladder from the stern of the ship.

Puzzled, I leaned over the coamings as the two swimmers now came alongside. I recognized Alex immediately. The girl was a stranger.

'Idioto!' José was muttering. 'Who would have a son like mine?' Then he went off into a whole stream of rapid Spanish which, from his tone, wasn't very flattering.

I peered with curiosity as Kevin helped, first the girl, then Alex aboard.

'We thought we'd come and join you,' Alex

announced, shaking his dripping hair all over the cockpit. 'Give you a surprise.'

José glared at his son, then started the engines and concentrated on heading the ship towards Andraitx harbour. Alex went over and clapped a hand on his father's back but, when there was no response, he shrugged his glistening shoulders and turned his attention to the girl who stood beside him. She was stunning, with waistlength jet-black hair, deeply tanned skin and an incredible figure which was silhouetted perfectly in a daringly cut-away white costume.

'This is Theresa.' Alex slipped his fingers round the girl's slim waist.

'Hello!' the girl lisped in broken English. Then she smiled and her small heart-shaped face was even more beautiful.

'Hi,' I said, trying to match her smile – and failing. I suddenly felt out-classed. Even if my baggy denim shorts and cut-off T-shirt were exchanged for Theresa's clinging one-piece, there was no way I'd ever look anything like her.

I glanced from Kevin to Alex, then over to José, they were all looking at Theresa who stood like some picturesque Greek goddess, risen from the waves.

'Anyone like a drink?' I spluttered, trying to break the silence.

Alex turned and smiled in my direction. 'Oh, hello?' he said as if he'd just realized I was on board. I felt his eyes begin to take in my bare legs and windswept hair, so I headed for the main hatchway.

I wasn't in the habit of being part of an inspection parade!

'Drinks?' I repeated, and got bombarded with orders.

Trying to remember who wanted what, I slipped down into the galley and stood staring at the fridge, trying to understand why I suddenly felt so immature and unsophisticated. I'd never felt that way before. Never. And now that I did, I didn't like it. And somehow it had everything to do with Alex.

I opened the fridge and took out three cokes – and a beer, for José. Then decided on a glass of water for myself. I was about to put them all on a tray, when I changed my mind and left my water on the worktop. It would be an excuse to come down later, on my own – and stay down, until we docked.

Are you crazy? I suddenly asked myself. Never in your sailing career have you ever stayed below decks when a boat docks. You're not going to start now.

I clambered up and handed round the drinks. José was talking animatedly to Alex, and Kevin was in deep conversation with Miss Greek Goddess. At least it wasn't so much a conversation as a lot of arm waving accompanied by giggles.

I watched them for a while before making my way towards the bow of the ship, watching the harbour come closer and closer. Seagulls swooped overhead, screeching for food, drifting on invisible currents. The quay along the harbour wall was busy with boating people and tourists. There was an air of excitement and enjoyment everywhere and I let myself be carried along with it.

'You look even more like a mermaid today,' Alex said, startling me.

I spun round, ready for a sparring match. But I suddenly became aware of the warmth from his body so close to mine that, for a moment, a wave of confusion clouded my thinking. Then I stepped back, away from him, distancing myself. 'Your girlfriend is waiting for you,' I stuttered.

'No she isn't,' came his amused reply. 'She's too interested in your brother. Besides, she's my ex-girlfriend.' He laughed as he saw the expression on my face. 'It's true,' he told me, amusement lighting his dark eyes. 'Don't look so suspiciously at me.'

I turned to walk away, but he barred my way with his arm.

'Why must you be so unfriendly?' he asked, his tone softer now.

He had a point there, but I was too confused to make a sane reply. So I simply replied, 'Am I?'

A frown puckered his brown forehead. 'Yes, you are. And for me, it is distressing.'

'I'm sorry,' I found myself saying.

He nodded, looking a little less concerned. 'You see, all the girls like me a lot. I want you to like me, too. I'm a nice guy.'

Oh ho, I thought, a small uneasy feeling pricking at the back of my mind, could this be stage two? It certainly was a new tack.

I smartened up, straightened up and side-stepped him. 'I'll take your word for it,' I told him. 'But that's all. I'm here to work on the *Goddess*, not get involved with anyone. No matter how nice he tells me he is, okay?'

The tight, sardonic look sprang back into his eyes. 'You're one very hard, cool lady,' he accused me.

'You bet I am!' I replied, then realizing the ship was already reversing into harbour, I hurried past him and went to locate the boat hook. After all, someone had to crew the *Goddess*, didn't they?

Chapter 6

The next few days were such a whirl of activity that I really didn't have much time to think about anything – let alone Alex Covas. Between taking the *Golden Goddess* out to get acquainted with her during the mornings, and then helping make inventories, and stocking the ship for her first charter, the days seemed to pass in a kind of haze. Mostly, it was just José, Kevin and I who took off in the early morning sunlight. Alex appeared to have other things to occupy himself with.

I saw a couple of them. The first one was sitting with him outside Donal's bar. She was a vivacious blonde, wearing a brilliant cerise-coloured playsuit; the other was riding pillion on his bike, her long, sun-streaked hair flowing out behind her bare, bronzed shoulders as he sped down the mountain road in front of us.

José didn't say anything on either occasion, but I noticed from the thin set of his lips that he wasn't happy.

When I'd mentioned it to Kevin, he'd shrugged, 'Good luck to him,' was all he said.

'Alex could at least try to help his father,' I'd pressed, growing angry with Kevin's attitude. He was taking sides, and he certainly wasn't on mine.

Kevin had stopped checking off the tinned provisions against his list, and looked at me quizzically.

'Hey, little sis, why are you so interested in what Alex does, anyway?'

'I'm not interested,' I'd thrown back, anger sharpening my words. 'As far as I'm concerned, he can do what he likes, the nerd! I just think he could be of more help to his father on the boat.'

Kevin had gone back to checking the list, but not before I'd noticed an amused expression light his blue eyes.

'And just what's so amusing?'

'You are, sis,' came the reply. 'For someone who's not interested, you spend a heck of a lot of time thinking and talking about Alex.'

'I don't know what you're on about,' I threw back.

'Don't you?' Kev didn't even bother looking at me. I ignored him.

On the way home to the villa on Friday, José told us how pleased he was with the way we worked.

'You're a great duo,' he praised. 'It's nice to have you two around. Alex prefers the pleasure side of sailing to the work and my lovely Rosie is not a practical person on a boat.'

I felt a bit embarrassed. I smiled at José then looked daggers at Kevin – loaded with 'I told you so'.

Trust Kevin to come out with the right reply. He might be eighteen but sometimes he talks like he's going on eighty!

'I guess we can't all like the same things in life, if we did, there'd be some mighty long queues.'

Laughter spluttered from José. 'You're right there. And, if I was honest, I'd admit I'm a bit possessive about the *Goddess*. I love every moment I'm on her and am not very happy away from her. That's why I choose to crew rather than get a skipper. I only charter her out because I want to share my enjoyment of her with others.'

'That's a lovely thought,' I said, and José grinned sheepishly.

'Don't give my secret away to anyone, will you?' he said. Kevin and I laughed, and promised his secret was safe enough.

As the Mercedes came to a halt outside the villa, Nelson, the family's large boxer-type dog came bouncing out, barking loudly. He was quickly followed by a petite girl dressed in tennis whites.

'Pilar!' José jumped from the car and proceeded to greet his daughter with warmth and affection. There were many hugs and a fountain of kisses, then more hugs, and a lot of happy laughter.

Eventually, his arm clasped tightly round the small girl's waist, José turned to introduce Kevin and me.

'This is my joy. The light of my life. My precious jewel,' José enthused.

Smiling, Pilar stepped out of her father's embrace and came forward to greet us. Well, to greet Kevin anyway. After giving me a brief, cursory nod, she started chatting Kevin up like boys were going out of fashion.

Kevin, drat him, lapped it up.

Great, I thought. This is going to be a wonderful holiday.

'And you play tennis, Kevin?' Pilar was enquiring in her charming, rather carefully pronounced English. 'And you dive with the snorkel and mask?' She seemed delighted when Kevin appeared to fill all her requirements. She turned to José who was following up the rear of our odd, assorted procession.

'Oh, Papa, it is wonderful! You have been so clever to get Kevin here this summer. Now I will have a lovely time. You know how bored I get with all the old people that normally come to charter.' Her dark eyes flashed mischievously, and her perfectly even white teeth shone as she chatted on, like machine-gun fire. 'Oh, this is going to be a perfect summer, I can feel it.'

José shook his head, indulgently, then turned to talk to me.

'You see? My daugher and her twin brother are the same. Fun lovers, both of them.'

I glanced in front. Pilar now had both arms hooked over Kevin's. She was hanging on to him and dancing along like a little girl. Only Kevin wasn't looking at her as if she were a little girl. Far from it!

Without meaning to, I let out an irritated sigh. Then quickly glanced sideways. José hadn't appeared to notice my annoyance. He was busy playing with Nelson as the dog ran alongside, jumping up repeatedly, only to be gently pushed away again.

Oh boy, I thought, not very kindly. This island is something else. Everyone seems to be ... I couldn't think of the word I was searching for. It evaded me. Then my mind clarified, and I thought, casual.

That's what it was. Casual. Everyone behaved as if they'd known each other all their lives. There was none of the detachment on meeting someone for the first time, here. I found it disturbing. All my instincts told me to play it cool when I met a new person. Take my time. Get to know them. Not jump in with both wellies on.

Kevin didn't seem bothered by the same set of feelings, at all. He laughed along with Pilar, obviously thoroughly enjoying himself. I wondered what Julia, his part-time girlfriend back home would say if she could see him now? Compared to his normal serious image, this new Kevin was a stranger. And that unnerved me, too. I wanted my brother to be the person I always knew and relied on. I wasn't sure if I liked this new version.

I followed the group into the house, lost in thought. I decided I'd have a word with brother Kev. Just to warn him.

About what? I heard a small voice inside my head ask.

67

I didn't bother to answer that one. I had the impression it could be far too complicated and confusing to try to fathom it all out. Anyway, I was starving and Marie-Carmen had prepared a huge platter of albondigas – small spicy meatballs – and a large jug of chilled San Francisco for our return. It was waiting for us on the patio table.

Pilar proceeded to help Kevin and herself.

I got my own.

'Are you crazy, Kevin?' I spluttered, later that night. 'It's ten-thirty and tomorrow we've to be on the ship at seven, and you're suggesting I go to the disco in Paguera?'

Kevin had rolled his eyes to the ceiling, then sunk down on my bed.

'We're young, kiddo,' he said. 'We're on a sort of holiday, and we've been invited.'

I plonked myself down beside him, my shoulders dropping. 'You're wrong, Kev, we're not on holiday, we're here to work. And, if you don't mind my correcting you, *you* have been invited, no one bothered to send me a printed invitation!'

'You're being childish,' came Kev's retort.

That really made me see red. 'I'm seventeen and I am not childish.' I jumped up and walked over to the terrace windows.

'You're sixteen until the end of this month, and you're acting like a six-year-old.' Kevin sounded cross, which only made me more belligerent. I tore my eyes away from the panoramic view of the mountains and sea and turned on him.

'And you've gone all funny since you came here.'

That floored him – his expression changed to one of puzzlement.

'What do you mean, funny?'

Okay, you asked for it, I thought, Here goes. I stood my ground, facing him squarely. Then, beginning to tick the points off on my fingers, I began.

'One, you're not like you normally are back home. Two, you're all over every girl that comes into view. Three, you ignore me and four. . . .'

But I didn't get to four because Kevin shot off the bed and paced across to confront me.

'That's about it, isn't it, Susan?' His face was about an inch away from mine. I stepped back.

'That's about what?' I didn't like the edge to his voice.

'You,' he said, levelly. 'Because *you* aren't the centre of attention all the time, you're behaving like a spoiled kid.'

'That's not true.' I found myself on the defensive.

'Yes it is. Normally, back at the club, you're about the only girl with all the fellas. There's no competition. And you may not realize it, but you love it. Well, here there's lots of competition and for once, you find yourself as part of the group. Only you can't handle it.' He turned and began walking from my bedroom. 'If I were you, kiddo,' he said, cuttingly, 'I'd wise up and stop reacting like a baby who's had its bag of sweets taken away. Life's about communicating. Mixing. If you don't, you'll find it's going to be a long, lonely holiday.'

'You're over the top, brother Kevin!' I called after

him. 'Totally wrong. Bankrupt in the top storey . . . ' my words faded as he shut the door firmly between us.

For a long while I stood quietly fuming in the middle of the room. Who on earth did he think he was, talking to me like that? He had to be suffering from sunstroke. In spite of my heated words, I began to feel a great wave of depression wash over me. I threw myself on the bed and grabbed fistfulls of pillow, burying my flushed face into the cool cotton. For some stupid, idiotic reason huge tears were falling down my cheeks.

I drew in a shuddering breath on a fresh burst of tears and thumped the pillow furiously. It was all *his* fault! That hateful nerd. It was all Alex's fault. Everything was.

And then I thought. Wait a sec. How come it's *his* fault? I rolled over and let out a gasp, while I stared unseeingly at the beamed ceiling. I was too confused. It was far too hot. And I was tired.

I won't try to work it out now, I told myself. I'll feel better in the morning. Then, I'll be able to see things clearly and explain to Kevin just why he is wrong. Tomorrow, everything will be better.

Only as it turned out, I was wrong. It was worse.

I was woken with a thumping headache. Oh boy! I thought groggily, sitting up and realizing something wasn't right. I peered at my bedside clock then, in panic, threw back the sheet. It was six-thirty.

'Why didn't you wake me up, rotter?' I blazed as

I met Kevin, washed and dressed, coming out of the bathroom as I made my way in.

'Now, is that a nice good-morning?' he asked, grinning infuriatingly.

I pushed past him. 'You're not a very nice person, letting me sleep late.'

'Forget it, we're not going down to the *Goddess* until eight. The flight time's been changed. The people who are chartering telephoned last night to say they won't be in Andraitx until this afternoon.'

'You could have told me!' I stormed.

'You would have heard it yourself if you'd been with us last night instead of sulking off to bed. We had a great time.'

I didn't bother to reply. I had an urge to hit him. As it was, I slammed the bathroom door shut between us then turned on the shower. Without testing the water, I stepped under it and nearly froze to the spot. The water was icy.

I gritted my teeth and began to furiously shampoo my hair which was sticky with sea water, and in a tangle. For a moment, I toyed with the idea of having it cut short. I'd seen a photograph in one of Mum's weekly magazines that I'd liked. The style was all sort of spikey in the front, and short at the back. But up until now, I hadn't really thought about it seriously.

After I'd rinsed off the conditioner, I stood in front of the mirror and played about, pulling my hair off my face and bunching it up in the front. I looked like a Cabbage Patch doll on a bad day. I peered at my reflection closer. There was a rather nasty looking mound deforming my nose. As my fingers carefully examined it, I winced. It hurt.

That is going to look like Mount Etna before lunchtime, I thought. I never get spots. Not normally. Only just before my period. Then I groaned out loud. It had never occurred to me. What a wonderful time to get the curse. On my first week of crewing. Fantastic!

I sank down on the bidet and covered my face with my hands and blanked my mind. If I'd thought about anything at that precise moment, I would have packed my bags and got the first flight home.

The wave of black misery threatened to grow worse. I hugged my knees up to my chest and wondered why I felt so rotten. It was all going wrong. Then I remembered Mum's favourite expression. She was always quoting it to us when problems came along. 'It's not the size of the problem that's important,' she'd say, 'it's the way we relate to it. If we get everything in perspective, that's half the problem solved.'

I thought about that for a while, then got up and went to clean my teeth, still thinking it over.

I was still thinking about the sense of it later when I walked out into the brilliant sunlight to have breakfast on the patio.

'I missed you last night.' Alex was sitting alone at the table.

I squinted my eyes against the glare to see him more clearly. He was studying me, waiting for my reaction, a wary look in his dark, liquid eyes.

I sat down on a bamboo chair opposite, and then reached for the coffee pot, unsure of what to say. . . .

'You would have enjoyed it.' Alex tried again. Then added, 'Why didn't you come?'

I shrugged as I poured coffee into a clean cup. 'I'm not a very good dancer,' I found myself admitting.

He didn't jump at the chance to laugh at me. Or make a joke at my expense. Instead, he smiled with what I could only describe as sympathy.

'I'm not very good, either,' he confided, which threw me.

'I can't believe that.' I eyed him suspiciously. 'I'm sure you must be good at everything.'

'There you go again.' Alex replaced his cup firmly on his saucer, then said, 'You make a big mistake with boys, Susan. You are afraid to let them be nice to you.' He began to look puzzled. 'Kevin told me you are not like this in England, so I must assume it is me you are afraid of.'

I squirmed in my seat. The conversation was becoming too personal. I told him that most certainly wasn't the case, and concentrated on finishing my coffee.

Alex studied me for a while longer before he leaned back and stretched his muscular legs in front of him.

'Well,' he seemed to be carefully choosing his words, 'I hope we can be friends on board the *Goddess* these next few weeks.' He grinned sheepishly, as if a sudden thought amused him. 'You know, it would be such a shame to waste time in such a romantic setting.' He leaned forward again, his elbows on the table, his chin in his hands, as he gazed across at me. 'I see the sun's brought you out in freckles,' he said. Then added, 'And a spot.'

My *ensaimada* nearly stuck in my throat. I spluttered violently. When I'd finally cleared my lungs, I fixed him with what I hoped was a cold, dismissive stare.

Only Alex didn't seem to notice because the very next second, he'd reached across, took hold of my fall of hair, and gently eased my head closer to his.

For one frightening second, I thought: He's going to kiss me! But the next second, his fingers flicked against my temple, then he released me.

'A flake of pastry' he explained, a questioning smile on his handsome face. He glanced at his watch, then stood up. 'I'd better round up the others,' he said. 'See you later.'

I sat and watched him, as if from a vast distance. Down the end of a swirling tunnel. Except the only thing that was swirling was my head, and my emotions. I still felt the gentleness of his touch. His warm fingers against my skin; the softly amused yet tender look in his eyes.

I was still reeling from the sudden and unexpected effect he'd had on me when I heard the chatter of excited voices. The next moment, Pilar and Kevin, their bodies glistening with water, plonked themselves on to seats either side of me.

'Do you not swim?' Pilar confronted me, her eyes darkly questioning – so like her brother's.

When I nodded, she seemed relieved. 'That's good. At least you won't be a wet blanket on board.'

I could have taken offence. Flown into fury at her

blunt remark. But I didn't because I caught sight of Kevin's worried expression. I smiled instead. Immediately, Pilar was off on her next topic of conversation. It was plain she hadn't meant to be personal.

After listening to her chatting on for a while, I realized she didn't purposefully ignore me. She was simply far too involved with her own conversation. In fact, listening to her hotchpotch type chatter I'd have said she wasn't really aware of anyone in particular. She just needed an audience. And Kevin, being Kevin, was a wonderful listener. He'd had good training. He'd been listening to me for sixteen years! Then I thought, maybe what Kevin had said the previous night had hit a sore point. Maybe his accusations had some truth to them. Maybe I had behaved badly because I'd been jealous.

Luckily, Rosie and José appeared on the terrace at that moment, so I couldn't confuse myself further with any in-depth self-analysis.

'You kids all packed and ready?' José asked, smiling across at me as he dropped a fatherly kiss on Pilar's upturned cheek.

I nodded, but realized Rosie was still in her housecoat. As if reading my thoughts, Rosie said, 'I've decided not to come on this first charter. It's only a married couple with one little girl, so there's enough of you to cope without me.'

Pilar let out a groan. 'But Mama,' she said, 'who will do the catering? You know I hate cooking in a galley.'

I was becoming aware that all heads were slowly

being turned on me. I gazed from one pair of eyes to another, then shrugged.

'Me?' I said. To my surprise Pilar jumped up, ran over and planted a kiss on both my cheeks.

'You are an angel!' she proclaimed happily. 'I shall love you for ever!'

Chapter 7

'Ready to fend off?' José called from the cockpit.

'Ready!' I shouted back, holding the boat hook and placing feet astride, steadying myself for safety.

'Do you want me to do that?' Alex asked, distracting me for a precious second from pressing the hook against the quay as I heard the engines of the *Golden Goddess* come to life.

'Grab another hook!' I instructed, angry that my proposed angle of leverage had been lost. I hurried forward to get another position.

I was vaguely aware of Alex blundering over the deck searching for the second boat hook, but refused to allow myself to be side tracked any more.

José sailed the boat in a broad arc until the anchor chain began to slacken, allowing Kevin who was at the stern to begin to haul it in.

Under José's guidance the *Golden Goddess* slowly and carefully began to tack and sail toward the anchor until Kevin completed the task of pulling it on board.

As usual when I felt the boat finally under way a wave of excitement rippled through me.

Some people on a nearby boat waved us off. We waved back. That's one of the great things about boating people, everyone has time for everyone else. It's like belonging to a world-wide club.

'Friends of yours?' Alex asked.

I secured the boathook back in its position, before turning my attention to him. He was dressed in white Bermuda shorts – and nothing else. His deeply-tanned body glistened with suntan oil and rippled with firm, hardened muscles.

I pointed to where Kevin was setting the headsail. 'Why not stop asking questions and go see if Kevin needs a hand?' I said, authoritatively. To my surprise, he gave a mock salute, then left.

'Are we going to meet some pirates?' a small voice piped up. I looked down as a hand tugged at my arm.

Rebecca was five. She was a gingerhead; two lines of freckles bridged her pert nose and she had huge hazel eyes. I'd loved her from the moment her parents had arrived for their three-week charter.

I frowned, pretended it was a very serious question. 'I shouldn't think so, Becky,' I said, 'but if we do there's no need to be afraid. We've four big men on board to protect us.'

Becky was pensive for a moment, then she beckoned me closer. I crouched beside her and she whispered, 'I want to meet a pirate, Susan. I saw a film about pirates on the TV. I'm not afraid of them! I think it would be fun.'

'In that case, I'll have a word with the skipper and see what we can arrange,' I told her, trying hard not to smile.

Becky put a finger to her lips. 'I won't tell anyone else. It will be our secret.'

I feigned a serious expression, then squeezed her tiny hand.

'Okay, it's our secret,' I confided.

She smiled a sweet smile, then said, 'I'm thirsty, can I have a fizzy drink?'

'Sure, come on. I'll take you to my tiny kitchen. It's stacked with a whole ton of wonderful goodies.'

Becky nodded, assuming a very adult expression for one so young. 'It should be,' she said, following at my side. 'My Daddy said it had cost him a fortune to hire the boat and he expected to be treated like a king.'

'Oh, did he?' I replied, surprised, but a bit put off by her innocent confession.

The small halo of ginger curls nodded. 'And Mummy said she doesn't want to be bothered with anything at all. She just wants to have a relaxing holiday.'

Holding Becky's small hand safely in mine I made my way towards the cockpit and main hatch. I had a strange feeling that Tom and Sheila Lloyd-Prentis were going to be a difficult couple to please. Still, looking on the brighter side of things, I realized that's what we were on board for. To help make other people's holidays on the *Goddess* memorable and happy. As I went below, I caught sight of Sheila Lloyd-Prentis – a mousey-looking woman with thin, angular features – relaxing on the bunk seats in the cockpit talking to José, who was at the helm. Her husband, dressed impeccably in crisp white slacks, short-sleeved shirt with epaulettes and a brand new sailing cap – covering what I'd noticed, was a completely bald head – stood importantly, legs astride, on the teak deck, his arms folded across his narrow chest. The image was certainly every inch a seafaring man. Every inch, that was, except for his face which seemed to be draining of colour with every second that passed.

I'd only been in the galley a couple of minutes when Tom Lloyd-Prentis's grey face appeared in the doorway.

'Where's the bathroom?' he asked, his voice hardly above a strained whisper.

I stopped foraging in the fridge and glanced up. 'The main head's off the saloon, before the master cabin.'

He looked confused. 'Head?' he queried, one hand creeping to his throat, then to his mouth.

'The head's the bathroom on a ship,' I informed him, wondering if he'd even make it. To my surprise he turned on me.

'Don't treat me like a fool, young lady!' he said. I think he might have said a whole lot more if José hadn't cut the *Goddess*'s engines at that precise moment and we immediately felt the full movement of the boat as we started to move forward under sail. Tom Lloyd-Prentis exited rapidly.

I busied myself with finding Becky a lemonade, then went aloft to take orders for drinks. Becky ran to sit beside her mother, 'I think Daddy's being sick,' she informed her mother, and the rest of the crew, in a loud, clear voice.

Sheila Lloyd-Prentis stifled a giggle, then tried to appear serious as she hushed her young daughter. 'Nonsense, Rebecca,' she said, 'your Daddy's a seasoned sailor. He's never sick.'

'He is!' the young girl argued. Then added, 'I'm not sick and nor is anyone else. Daddy's the only one.' She paused, looking puzzled. 'What's a seasoned sailor?' she asked.

'It doesn't matter, poppet,' her mother told her.

I caught sight of Pilar's face. She was trying not to giggle, which nearly started me off. I had a feeling that this was going to be a very interesting cruise.

José sailed the *Goddess* through calm, blue seas as far as Puerto Soller before we dropped anchor, for lunch. I busied myself with preparing a large salad from the provisions we'd brought on board and then made mushroom-and-cheese omelettes. Despite the well-ventilated galley, by the time I'd flipped the last omelette on to a plate, I was feeling hot and sticky, if not a bit claustrophobic.

'I shall prepare the puddings,' Alex announced, as he helped to carry the food through to the table in the main saloon.

'That's nice of you,' I said politely. I wasn't quite sure how to react with the new Alex. Ever since we'd set sail he'd seemed different. Almost normal. But I still didn't trust him.

Now, he placed the plate he'd carried through to Sheila Lloyd-Prentis, before seating himself beside her.

'I like a man who can cook,' Mrs Lloyd-Prentis said, smiling at Alex under heavily-mascaraed lashes. 'There's nothing like a good male cook, I always say.'

Alex glanced uncomfortably across at me. I raised my eyebrows, amused by yet another of his conquests.

Next to me, I felt her husband bristle.

'You say a lot, Sheila, and mostly it's totally inconsequential.' He turned to me, and in the same harsh tone said, 'I hope these omelettes were made with fresh, not dried eggs?'

'Of course they are fresh eggs!' Pilar cut across. She wagged a finger at Tom Lloyd-Prentis as if she were, for all the world, scolding a naughty boy. 'You must not make any comment about Susan's cooking. She is a wonderful cooker.'

I started to giggle, picturing me as an upright gas stove.

'The word is cook – or chef,' Kevin corrected her, trying to keep a straight face, too. But he started laughing anyway – mostly I think from nerves. Tom Lloyd-Prentis had that effect on you. Luckily, Becky started spluttering and then laughing and finally, even her parents couldn't hold out any more and started smiling, too.

The rest of the lunch went off well enough – especially when Alex brought in an impressive tray of ice-cream-filled oranges. I toyed with the idea of deflating his ego by telling everyone he was a cheat.

He hadn't made them at all. I'd loaded a whole box of assorted ice-cream filled fruits into the deep freeze only yesterday.

'Local picked oranges,' he announced, handing one to Becky, who looked wide-eyed with wonder. 'And the ice-cream is made from our own cows' milk.'

I glared at him – he glared back, challenging me to contradict. But as Tom Lloyd-Prentis actually looked happy with the story, I decided to keep my mouth shut and my thoughts to myself.

'How're they settling in?' José asked, in low tones as we sat on the deck later that afternoon.

I'd been stitching a button on a pair of shorts, and now smiled ruefully. 'Mr Lloyd-Prentis felt sick again after lunch, and went off to lie down. Sheila and Becky are having a swim with the others.' I peered over the side. The five of them were playing around on a couple of bright yellow Lilos near the stern of the *Goddess*. The water looked so inviting I was tempted to go in myself, except that was out of the question as my period was heavy.

'They seem an odd-matched couple,' José mused, half to himself.

I nodded, watching as he checked a chart, open on the deck in front of him. Having satisfied himself about something, he began to carefully fold it up.

'Where are we making for next?' I asked. We'd discussed the proposed passage already, but I'd forgotten most of the strange-sounding names.

'Pollensa,' he reminded me. 'But not until tomorrow. For the rest of today we'll stay around

Soller. If our guests like to go ashore this evening, to see a bit of the port and take a trip up to the old town, you could go with them.'

'I don't think so,' I said.

'Why ever not?' José looked suprised. 'You'll love it. The town's so different from the port. The towns were built mostly several kilometres in from the sea to confound invaders – give the locals time to rally their defences in case of attack.' He smiled across at me. 'If you remember your history, Susan, you should know that many Mediterranean islands were constantly under attack from one source or another. Nowadays, of course,' he said, pensively, 'it is the tourists who are the invaders.'

I glanced towards the coastline . . . past the yacht harbour with its collection of gleaming masts, glinting in the heat of the afternoon, up past the rugged, pine covered mountains to where the bottle-green foliage met starkly with the deep sapphire sky.

'The island's so beautiful' I remarked. 'I can understand people wanting to capture it for themselves.'

Before José could make any remark, a loud, piercing scream shattered the tranquillity of the still air.

Dropping my sewing I raced to the side of the boat. A pair of thin, pale arms were thrashing about in the water very near the side of the boat.

Without stopping to think, I grabbed the lifebuoy and pitched it over the edge, then climbed over the grab rail and dived in.

I clasped Becky and slipped one arm under her chin. To my surprise she pushed away, laughing!

'It's a joke. It's a joke,' she spluttered. 'I wasn't drowning. I was playing.'

I let go of her and trod water, not knowing whether to laugh – or hit her. One thing was certain, I wasn't going to waste any more time in the sea.

'Swim round to the ladder and climb aboard.' My voice was cold and authoritative.

She shook her wet curls at me. Her bottom lip stuck out obstinately.

'Get out of the water,' I repeated. This time, the threat in my voice must have got through because she began swimming strongly towards the stern of the boat.

I grabbed the lifebuoy and swam after her. As she began to pull herself up, I was right behind her.

'She all right?' Alex asked from behind me as I stepped, soaking wet, and furious on to the deck.

I nodded, bending over to get my breath back. I wrung the water out of my ponytail, then stood up.

Becky was sullenly watching me.

'You don't ever do that again,' I scolded her. 'It is silly and could be dangerous. For you and others. Understand?'

A voice from the hatchway made me spin round. Becky's father was standing there, still ashen faced except for two bright scarlet patches on his cheeks.

'How dare you talk to my daughter like that!' he demanded. 'Who are you to reprimand her? I pay you to look after us, not dictate what we should or should not do.'

I was so shocked, I simply stood, open mouthed. But though I couldn't bring myself to reply, Alex did. And how! He really let rip. By the time he had explained in detail just how senseless and hazardous the whole prank was, both father and daughter were standing silently. José who had observed everything, looked impressed with his son.

Alex finally turned to me. 'Go down and change, Susan, you look exhausted,' he said, gently, but sternly. 'Then if I were you, I'd have a rest. You've had enough shocks for one day.'

I didn't argue. I was only too happy for Alex and José to sort everything out with the Lloyd-Prentises. I don't know whether it was the shock, or the fact that I'd hit the water at the wrong angle, or simply the heat, but I suddenly felt weak and terribly tired.

I went to the head, showered, dried myself, then took myself to my bunk in the small, rather cramped fore-cabin which I shared with Pilar. Within minutes I was lulled into a deep, dreamless slumber.

I woke after six, aware that Pilar was in the cabin. I rolled over and smiled at her.

'You are feeling better?' she asked, sitting down on the bunk opposite.

'Yes, thanks,' I told her. She looked pert and pretty in a flared red skirt and white, off-the-shoulder blouse.

'Good! Then get up and put on something nice. We are all going ashore,' she instructed me.

'Not me, Pilar,' I told her, explaining 'I've a terrible headache, and besides, my tummy aches.'

She looked alarmed and moved across to sit on my bunk. 'You are sick! This is terrible. Who will cook?'

I had to laugh at her. She was so blunt about everything. 'I'm fine – just the usual monthly problems, you understand?'

She frowned, then suddenly looked immensely relieved. 'Are you sure?' I nodded, but her glossy eyes scrutinized me more closely. 'I think that is not the whole truth. I think it is because of my brother. You do not like him. He told me.'

'He did?'

Pilar nodded, then gave a small sigh. 'But it is his own fault. He thinks all girls fall in love with him at once.' She giggled. 'Mostly, you understand, they do. But I told him, I said, Alejandro, Susan is English. She is different to the Spanish girls. She will not fall for you – whoosh! – like that. You English are cold. You have to be sure about your feelings. That is right, is it not?'

I was sitting up now, my eyes wide with surprise and amusement.

'You told him all that?' Pilar nodded. 'What did he say?' I was curious.

Pilar's tongue clicked against her teeth. 'What he always says. To mind my own business.' She stood up and began frantically to search round – locating one, then a second, scarlet pump, before she turned back to me. 'Won't you change your mind?' she pleaded. When I again refused, she shrugged nonchalantly. 'Alex will be very angry,' she told me. 'But it will do him good. He hurts too many girls. Every week there is another. He doesn't care.'

'Hasn't he ever had a serious girlfriend?' I asked, curious.

'The girlfriends are serious – but he, never! He says he has not met the right girl yet. Now, if you are not changing your mind, I am going. Oh,' she added as an afterthought, 'Becky will be on board so you could look in on her.'

I shook my head, settling back on my pillow. 'Tell them I'm sorry. And don't worry about Becky. I'll babysit.'

Pilar swirled round and opened the cabin door. 'I'll tell them – but Alex will sulk, you'll see.' Then with a flash of scarlet skirt and a happy giggle, she left.

I lay back in my bunk, closed my eyes and thought of what Pilar had said about Alex. Would he really care that I wasn't with them tonight, I wondered? Or would it just be his pride that was wounded? It had to be his pride, I told myself. Besides, what did I care? He meant nothing to me.

But why should he tell Pilar I didn't like him? Oh, it was all too muddled. I wasn't used to problems about boys. In fact, I'd never had any problems with any boy I'd ever known. They'd all been easy to understand, and to talk to. Just like being with Kevin, I thought. But that's where the difference lay. Alex in no way resembled Kevin. He was an enigma. That's what he was, I decided, feeling pleased with myself for identifying what he was. I thumped my pillow and tried to sleep. But I couldn't. Enigmas were very confusing. And I was certainly confused!

Chapter 8

Pilar had been right. Alex did sulk. Well, I assumed he was sulking as he seemed to go out of his way to avoid me. It was really silly, because even on a ship as big as the *Goddess*, the space is relatively small. But every time it looked as if we'd be alone together, Alex would make a special point of walking away.

I did manage to thank him for taking my part over Becky's prank, but he simply shrugged his shoulders, dismissively.

'Don't thank me,' he'd replied, coldly, 'I'd have done the same for anyone. It wasn't particularly for you.'

I'd been tempted to tell him to forget I'd mentioned it, but I didn't. I was also going to ask him what was eating him? And tell him he was behaving like a spoilt kid himself. But I stopped myself. One thing that's very important on board any ship is a happy, harmonious atmosphere. All my sailing life, that had been instilled in our minds by Dad. Just because an overgrown kid was behaving like his best cricket bat had been pinched didn't mean I had to behave in a similar fashion.

Anyway, for some perverse reason, I was amused that someone as self-assured as Alex Covas appeared to be annoyed because of my not falling in with his plans. Yet, at the same time, there was a small niggling feeling that made me uneasy. The fact was, I wasn't trying to be unfriendly. And to be honest, I didn't dislike Alex. I guess I was just a bit unsure of how I felt. Plus, I hadn't forgotten what Rosie had said about his reputation for the one, two, three act he adopted with most girls. Something Pilar had endorsed. I was going to make very sure that I didn't get trapped in the same net.

As it turned out, the cruise from Soller up along the coastline to Formentor, then round to the picturesque, natural harbour of Pollensa, was pretty hairy. What started out as a nice leisurely sail with a westerly wind carrying us along under sail past Valldemosa — made famous by Chopin and the writer, George Sand — suddenly changed as a fierce wind sprang up completely altering the weather. The Force Three wind whipped up into a Force Six within half an hour. It caught us off-guard and we found ourselves all on deck, battling like mad to trim the sails. The wavelets, only minutes before gentle with crests breaking away, became huge waves. The whole sea was a turbulent whirlpool, covered in white spray which was blown in streaks across the breakers.

Tom Lloyd-Prentis turned as white as the spraying foam and disappeared below decks. His wife quickly followed, pulling an excited and reluctant Becky after her. I found myself wondering why he'd bothered with the holiday. He wasn't a good sailor, and his temper seemed to grow worse with each passing day. I felt sorry for his wife. No wonder she was so timid.

But my mind didn't have a chance to wander far. I was too occupied with helping Kevin with the storm jib. As the wind was blowing along the course José wanted to take, he decided to sail downwind. I was surprised we made reasonable speed under the small jib, but we did.

Once or twice as I went round checking everything was well stowed and lashed down, I found Alex watching me.

'You don't seem at all worried,' he shouted above the howl of the wind as he helped me on one occasion with a loose cockpit locker.

I pushed strands of hair which were being wind-whipped into my eyes, off my face, and laughed.

'When you've been brought up sailing in British waters, you get used to bad weather. This is nothing compared to some gales we've found ourselves in.'

'You're a very surprising girl,' he'd called back, then added, 'And very brave.' I thought I'd detected a note of sarcasm in his voice.

'Not in the least,' I'd retorted. 'Just boat crazy. It gets in your blood.'

'Not in mine, it doesn't!' Alex had assured me as the wind sent another wave crashing over the side, spraying us with foam.

'You don't find this exhilarating?' I'd called.

'I find many things exhilarating. Trying to keep my balance on a heaving boat while Nature is trying to out-do herself around me is not one of them.'

I'd laughed – then realized he wasn't amused.

'Well, we can't all like the same things, as my brother Kev always says,' I told him.

Alex hadn't bothered to continue our conversation, he'd been too busy clinging on to the wet handrail, trying desperately to keep his feet firmly planted on the soaking deck. It crossed my mind that he actually looked scared, which didn't go with his sophisticated image.

By the time we reached Pollensa the wind had dropped to a light breeze, and the sun shone brightly, turning the water on deck to vapour. Kevin and Pilar busied themselves swabbing down, while I went below to check everything was okay.

'Where are our passengers?' I enquired, some time later, as I watched José and Alex take turns at pumping the water out of the bilges.

José grinned, wickedly. 'Ashore, where else? They were so delighted to see land, they almost ran down the gangplank.'

'Why do they charter if they don't like sailing?' I asked.

José shrugged. 'Many people like the idea of sailing. But the idea, and the reality are two different things.' He stepped back from the pump and slipped a protective arm round my shoulders. 'Not everyone is a natural-born sailor,' he told me. 'But you are. And so's that brother of yours.'

I felt, rather than saw Alex glance my way. I began to feel a bit awkward. Without actually saying so, it was clear José was implying that his son wasn't. Which, from what I'd seen, was true. but I couldn't really understand why. If my father had a ship like the *Goddess* and lived in such a fantastic place as

Mallorca, I'd be living on board nearly all the year round.

As if reading my thoughts, José said,

'Unfortunately, my two children prefer having their fun on land, not at sea.' There was a sharp, accusatory edge to his words. Alex must have recognized it. But he didn't rise to the bait, just continued pumping the water which the rough weather had brought to the bilges.

José's original passage had been planned with an overnight stay in Pollensa, then an early start on our course to the neighbouring island of Menorca, but Tom Lloyd-Prentis informed us he'd changed his mind.

'I think it would be better to stay around Pollensa for a few days,' he announced over dinner. When he noticed the looks exchanged between José and Kevin, he added, 'My wife isn't feeling too well after our dangerous and terrifying experience of getting here—'

'But I'm fine, Tom,' Sheila cut in, then stopped under her husband's withering stare.

'I know what's best for you,' he told her. 'We'll maybe cruise round Cabo del Pilar, to the bay of Alcudia, but nothing hazardous.'

'Pinar,' Alex corrected him. Then, explained, 'The correct name is, Cabo del Pinar not Pilar.'

'Are you trying to make me look small?' Tom Lloyd-Prentis glared at each of us in turn. I couldn't help thinking that he was managing to do that all by himself.

'Not at all,' Alex replied, politely. He stood up and walked from the saloon, steely faced.

Becky, who had been silently eating her fish and chips, suddenly stood up, too. Tears were welling in her hazel eyes and her bottom lip trembled.

'I don't want to stay on this ship any more!' she announced, her voice choked with tears. 'You are so horrid, Daddy. You are nasty to everyone. I want to go home.'

With that, she turned and ran towards the main hatch.

I swallowed hard to stop myself from saying I agreed with her every word. Instead, I excused myself and left the table, too.

Becky, I discovered, was huddled on the bank seats of the cockpit with Alex. He had his arm round her narrow shoulders as he talked softly to her.

When he heard me approach he glanced up, but didn't greet me. He carried on talking gently to the small girl.

'Tell you what, Becky,' Alex was saying. 'How about you and me slipping ashore early in the morning like invading pirates on an exploratory expedition? See what the natives are like?'

The sobs subsided. Two large eyes peered at Alex through wet lashes. 'What . . . what if Daddy won't let me?' she asked, tremulously.

Alex scratched his chin. 'Well, we could bribe him by saying we'll buy fresh *ensaimadas*, and bread. Then after we've bought the shopping we'll go explore the old town.'

Becky turned to me. 'Will you come, too, Susan?' A glint of excitement lit her eyes.

I hesitated for a moment, but the expression on Alex's face willing me to agree, left me with no way out.

So I smiled brightly, and agreed to join in their small adventure.

It was only later, as I tried to get to sleep in my cramped bunk, that I wondered just what I had done. I have to be mad, I thought, agreeing to go anywhere with Alex. Then I thought, what am I afraid of? It is just going to be a trip ashore with the son of my boss and a little girl. Not a commitment. Or was it? I finally fell asleep, confused but strangely excited.

A misty haze covered the water as Alex steered the small inflatable dinghy into Pollensa harbour. High overhead, lost in the arc of clear blue sky, seagulls called their morning greetings as the fishermen brought in the night catches. There was a feeling of newness everywhere. The air, already warm, promised another scorching day ahead.

Becky, looking like a small, pink-faced doll in her pretty blue playsuit, kept wriggling round on her seat, asking a million questions.

I glanced at Kevin and Pilar who had decided to accompany us and found myself thinking how well-matched they were. They'd grown very close during their time together and although Pilar was as chatty as ever, a new softness lit her dark eyes when she looked at Kevin.

'We can't make the invasion last too long,' Alex

told Becky. 'We're sailing round the bay to Alcudia after lunch.'

This didn't seem to worry Becky in the least. Her excitement at being away from her parents was almost tangible. Alex glanced across at me.

'It will have to be a lightning tour. We'll grab a cab and take in the old town then shop for provisions in the port afterwards.'

I smiled lazily, feeling happy and ready to fall in with any suggestion. It was such a perfect day.

'Count us out,' Pilar told Alex, as we clambered up on to the quay. 'I'm going to show Kevin round Pollensa myself. We'll rendezvous here at noon.'

Alex made a comment in Spanish which made Pilar blush prettily. She was clearly longing to have my brother all to herself for a while.

We waved them off then, with Becky between us, hanging on to our hands gleefully, we ran across the busy, noisy concrete esplanade to hail a black and white taxi.

The drive to the rambling old town of Pollensa took us past an impressive range of granite and pine-topped mountains. The town itself, about ten minutes away from the port, sat in the shadow of a huge peak which Alex told us was Mount Puig.

The sun was strong now, casting pitchy shadows from street corners and under stone arches. Green shutters at doors and windows gave a closed, almost austere appearance to the tiny, narrow streets, while here and there splashes of scarlet geraniums, or a cascade of purple bougainvillea colourfully con-trasted against old stones.

'Those are the famous Calvary Steps,' Alex told a wide-eyed Becky and me as we slowly drove along. 'There are 365 – one for each day of the year.'

'Can we walk up them now?' Becky pleaded, but Alex said we didn't have time.

'On Good Friday there's a candlelit procession all the way up to the old church at the top,' he explained proudly. 'It's very beautiful.' A smile suddenly touched his lips as he added, 'Like the two ladies I'm with today. Very beautiful.'

I didn't answer, just peered back at the mountain of shallow, age-worn steps flanked by dark cypresses and hoped Alex hadn't noticed my cheeks growing pink under my tan.

We stopped briefly by a souvenir shop while the taxi driver had a coffee in a bar. It was a virtual Aladdin's cave, full of bright ceramic plates, olive wood bowls and miniature dolls dressed in flamenco dresses.

Becky's eyes lit up with longing as she studied one raven-haired dancer dressed in a frilled and flounced pink and black costume. Before I had a chance to buy it for her, Alex had.

'And this one's for you, little mermaid,' he teased, handing me two dolls – a man and a woman – dancing together in a typical flamenco pose.

I stared at the intricate details of the white, lace-trimmed dress; at the man's velvet bolero and wide-brimmed hat sitting on top of his proud, handsome face – it looked so much like Alex that I didn't know what to say.

Becky, having made an assortment of exclamations

of delight, suddenly threw her small arms round Alex and kissed him loudly on the cheek.

'It's the most beautiful doll I've ever seen. Oh, thank you!' She hugged it to her with delight.

Alex glanced at me.

'Do I get such a warm thank you from you, too?' His eyes danced with anticipation.

I opened my mouth to say a polite thanks, but nothing came out. The words were stuck in my throat. The next second, Alex leaned over and before I could move, he'd touched my lips warmly with his. Then he was watching me, smiling tenderly – while I stood dazed and still speechless, and peculiarly dizzy from the effect of his lips brushing mine. If he was aware of my confusion, he didn't show it. He just turned and led us back to the waiting taxi.

By the time we had explored the shops back in the port of Pollensa – bought fresh provisions and the required *ensaimadas*, Kevin and Pilar were waiting for us on the quay.

'Come on, I'll treat us all to ice-creams,' Kevin announced, his arm round Pilar's bare midriff.

The idea of an ice was too tempting to say no to, so we all trooped happily along to the bright green-and-white decorated shop and sat at a pavement table, under a sun umbrella.

'I wish I'd brought my camera,' I moaned, a bit later, looking round the table. We were all hidden by the biggest ice-cream sundaes I'd ever seen. The glasses were like goldfish bowls!

'I'll remind you next year when you come back.'

Alex's voice was matter-of-fact. His dark eyes challenging over the top of his strawberry alaska.

'If there is ever a next time,' I remarked, coolly. He had a nerve, assuming so much.

'Oh, there will be,' he flipped back. 'I intend making sure of that.'

I became aware of Kevin and Pilar studying us as they held hands under the table. Even Becky's eyes were questioning the sparring match about to begin again.

I opened my mouth to argue, then shut it. It seemed silly and pointless when it was such a perfect day and I felt so happy, yet tingly with a new, inexplicable excitement. So I simply lowered my eyes, then plunged my long-handled spoon into the banana split I'd ordered.

Chapter 9

The message was waiting for Tom Lloyd-Prentis a week later when we sailed back from Menorca. The harbour master brought it to the *Goddess*, informing José that Tom had to contact London, on urgent business.

To say that the news brought a reaction would be an understatement. Tom Lloyd-Prentis went into a rage.

'How dare the firm contact me while I'm on holiday?' he stormed. 'I'll sack the lot of them. A man doesn't succeed by being surrounded by imbeciles.'

Still storming and ranting, he'd gone ashore with José to telephone London.

Oh, I do hope it isn't bad news,' Sheila Lloyd-Prentis said, downing her third gin-and-tonic in under half an hour. 'Tom has made so many enemies, so quickly,' she added morosely.

I glanced from Kevin to Alex as we sat round the saloon. Pilar was playing with Becky on board.

'He was such a different man before inheriting my father's textile business,' Sheila continued. She smiled tentatively across at me. 'But now he's become impossible! It's true I'm afraid. It's all an act – the Rolls, the big house, even this cruise . . .' she tailed off and went back to studying her empty glass. Finally, she sighed loudly, stood up and poured herself another drink.

I hardly recognized the man who climbed back on board the *Goddess* as the same man who'd left, only an hour before.

'What happened?' I asked Kevin, later, when we were alone.

Kevin shook his head, giving a small, nonchalant shrug. 'Something about Tom Lloyd-Prentis being voted off the company board in his absence. A sort of boardroom coup, or something just as traumatic. He said he's flying back to London immediately.'

'How?' I asked, knowing the airport was at the south of the island.

'Alex is hiring a car and driving them down.'

'And the boat?'

Kevin gave a wicked grin. 'We'll just have to sail her without the Lloyd-Prentises down to Andraitx ready for the next charterers, I'm afraid.'

I joined in Kevin's controlled delight. It was awful to admit it, but the idea that it would be just José and us on board made me very happy.

Then I realized Alex wouldn't be with us, and the bubble of happiness deflated a bit.

'Will Alex join us along the coastline?' I asked. Kevin shook his mop of thick hair and as his penetrating glance met mine, I looked away. I didn't want him to see what I was feeling. It was too private.

Sailing the *Golden Goddess* down the opposite coastline was something else. We had the most perfect weather and, as we weren't in a hurry, we made stops at nearly all the pretty harbours – from Cala Ratjada, along the emerald-green Costa de los Pinos to Porto Cristo; then from Cala Murada, down to the pretty little town of Cala d'Or, where we moored overnight in the picture-postcard clear waters of the little cove.

By the time we finally rounded Es Pontás, and sailed past Palma – its old Cathedral towering impressively against an azure sky – we were golden brown, and totally at home on the *Goddess*. I felt so confident in fact, that when José suggested I took over the helm, I didn't even hesitate. It was only afterwards I quaked when I realized I'd been the skipper of a sixty-three-foot motor-sailer. I couldn't wait to tell my mates back at the sailing club about that!

And, for good measure, I made Kevin take a photo, just for proof.

Rosie was waiting on the quay when we brought the *Goddess* in, under power.

'I've been so lonely. I refuse to be left at home on my own again,' she announced after showering kisses all round. 'Look at the colour of you!' she exclaimed. 'You're almost black!'

I surreptitiously glanced round, wondering if Alex was about. I didn't have to look far past her — he was lounging against the hull of a ship in dry dock, chatting to two girls. When he glanced up and saw me, he waved — but I turned my back on him.

Why on earth had I expected him to have changed? Just because he'd begun to be nice to me back in Pollensa, I told myself, didn't mean a thing. I suddenly felt an idiot. Fancy being taken in by his Stage Two – get the emotions going strategy! I'd had too much sun, I decided as I squarely turned my back on the whole boring scene. Let him get on with his flirting. I was here to work – not fall in love, like my big brother had with Pilar.

The following few days flew by. Cleaning and checking over the *Goddess* was tiring business and as she was such a big ship, it meant we were all kept working most of the time. Finally, when the new provisions had been stored, fresh water pumped aboard, linen changed, the sails inspected and the twin engines overhauled, I felt as if I needed a holiday!

'How would you like to teach the two teenagers who are coming with their parents to sail?' José asked.

We were relaxing on board the *Goddess* the evening before their arrival.

I stretched, feeling tired but happy. 'Fine by me,' I told him.

'Good. In that case we'll take along the mast to drop into the dinghy. It should keep the boys from getting bored,' José announced. 'Last year they were a bit of a handful.'

'How old are they?' I asked, wondering what I'd let myself in for.

José glanced at Rosie. 'How old are Jason and Mark?'

Rosie pondered for a second, then shrugged. 'Can't remember. Probably about fifteen, sixteen.' She ran her beautifully manicured fingers through her mass of hair as she sat watching the first diamond-bright stars appear in the darkening sky. 'Do they want to sail to Morocco again this year?' Rosie asked, turning her attention on her husband.

'Alice wants to, but Clifford always changes his mind at the last moment.' José glanced at his watch, then stood up. 'Well, come on all those who want to sleep in a real bed for the last night before we sail.'

The idea of a warm soak in a real bath, a good night's sleep where I could stretch out and not scrunch my feet against anything hard and unyielding, sounded like heaven.

'What are you two kids doing?' Rosie asked, directing her question towards Kevin and Pilar who were sitting with their heads close together, their feet dangling over the stern.

'I'm taking Kevin round to La Mola for a midnight swim,' Pilar replied.

'You'll be home before midnight. We've an early start in the morning,' Rosie told her.

Pilar giggled. 'Oh, Mama, you're such a pain. I'm eighteen, remember?'

'I'm not going to forget it. You'll be in by midnight – no arguments.'

'I'll make sure we are back,' Kevin assured her.

'And what about you, Susan?' Rosie glanced across at me. 'You going to join them at La Mola?'

I shook my head. 'No. I don't think so.'

'But you must!' Pilar sounded quite annoyed. 'Alex and everyone else will be there.'

'That's just why I'm not going,' I replied.

Pilar looked puzzled. 'What do you mean?'

'Susan means she's tired and wants an early night.' Rosie turned to me. 'Isn't that what you meant?'

I nodded, realizing that even if her daughter hadn't twigged why I was reluctant to join the group, Rosie had. Silently, I thanked her. She must have decided I was safer away from her charming, handsome, heartbreaking son. It never occurred to me to ask myself why she was so concerned. I only found that out later.

'I'm so sorry,' Kevin said the following morning as we all sat round the patio table, for breakfast. He

103

was nursing a heavily bandaged hand, and was looking very upset.

José shook his head, his lips a tight line. 'It can't be helped,' he said. 'Accidents happen to all of us. We don't go out looking for them.'

'It is Pilar's fault,' Rosie said, darting an accusing look at her daughter. 'She knows it is dangerous to swim in the sea at night. Even in a well-lit pool, it can be asking for trouble."

Pilar chewed on her bottom lip, but didn't reply.

'Pilar did warn me,' Kevin said, jumping to her defence. 'But I guess I wanted to show off – and dived in the wrong place. Luckily, it was only my hand that got damaged.' He let out an exasperated sigh. 'I don't know what to say, except I am truly sorry.'

'Well, you won't be able to crew, that's for sure,' José announced, not without sympathy. 'So Alex will have to. You will stay at home. Marie-Carmen will look after you.'

'I'll stay with him.' Pilar glanced from her mother to her father, then quickly added, 'Someone will have to drive him down to the medical centre to have his dressing changed, and Marie-Carmen can't drive, remember?'

'Pilar's right, José,' Rosie said, conclusively. 'She will have to stay here and Alex must crew.'

I glanced across at Alex who was toying with his large cup of black coffee. He hadn't said anything since I'd joined them for breakfast, but on a couple of occasions, when our eyes had met, I could see he was sulking again. Which somehow made me want to laugh. But I didn't.

Now he most certainly wasn't sulking. His expression was one of sheer panic.

'I can't crew, Papa!' he said. 'I'm hopeless on boats, you know that. You're always telling me, remember?'

'So, now's the time to alter my opinion,' José replied. 'You're going to have an admirable teacher.' He turned to me. 'That's if Susan doesn't mind teaching *three* kids?'

I didn't make a comment. I didn't dare. I felt Alex's eyes drilling into the back of my head.

'That's settled then,' Rosie announced, reaching for her coffee. Her green eyes settled on me, then the next second, she winked. 'It will make a change for a girl to teach *you* something, Alex, won't it?' she said, laughing softly to herself as she sipped her drink.

A Force Five easterly wind was blowing most of the way as we sailed south. The *Goddess*, happy with her sails billowing, covered the fifty miles across the Mediterranean to Morocco easily. It was the longest distance I'd ever sailed but with Alice and Clifford White keen, if not very proficient, sailors themselves, it was a happy ship. Happy, that was, except for Alex.

'You don't have to come in the dinghy,' I'd told him, early on. 'You make it obvious you hate it.'

'That's not true.' We were washing up in the galley, and I was trying to let him off the hook. Not that he seemed aware of it, from the way he'd carried on.

'I can't force you to learn to sail,' I'd continued.

'I'd prefer it if it were just you and me in the boat,' Alex had said, suggestively. 'But to have to be taught along with two kids.'

I'd laughed at that. 'Jason and Mark are only a year or so younger than you, Alex.'

'They're still kids.' He'd sounded like a spoiled child himself.

I'd plonked a freshly washed plate into his hands. 'Well, at least they try to understand the basics – not spend the time making silly remarks.'

'Is that what you think? That I'm silly?' His eyes had sparked dangerously.

I'd decided to play safe, and said nothing.

'Anyway, have you any idea how stupid that Mark looks, making eyes at you all day long? He's more interested in your legs than the rigging.'

I'd stared at him, open-mouthed. 'What? Don't be stupid! That's the most ridiculous, crazy, childish thing to say!' I blurted out – but I discovered I was talking to myself. Alex had walked out.

'He's jealous,' Rosie had announced, amusement making her pretty face even younger. She'd walked further into the galley, and lifted up the drying-cloth Alex had dropped. 'I'd never have believed it if I hadn't seen and heard it all. My son's certainly met his Waterloo with you. I'm so happy!'

'Rosie, that's nonsense. Alex doesn't see me as anything but a possible candidate for his One, Two, Three-Game Set and Match routine.'

Rosie had pulled a wry face, and concentrated with overdue care on the melamine plate she was drying. 'Maybe,' she conceded. 'But I'm not too sure this time. I'm really not.' She'd given me an awkward smile before putting the plate aside. 'He's changed, somehow.'

I didn't have time to dwell on Rosie's words because at that moment Mark had poked his head round the galley door.

'The skipper said to tell you we're approaching Ceuta Bay.'

'I'll be right up,' I'd replied, expecting him to run up on deck to pass on my message. But he'd continued to linger, smiling openly at me. Which had made *me* suddenly awkward as I'd recalled what Alex had said.

'Go and tell the skipper I'm on my way up,' I'd said, adding, '*now*. On board, you don't wait to be told anything twice. It could cost lives.'

'Oh, sorry, Susy,' he'd replied, using the pet name he'd adopted which, up till then, hadn't bothered me.'

'And Mark,' I'd called after him, 'my name's Susan.'

I'd heard his footsteps falter, then carry on. If he did have a crush, I'd decided I was about to get him out of it as easily and quickly as possible. Complications I didn't need – well, not more than I had already.

Mooring the *Goddess* in what appeared to be a choked, wall-to-wall mass of fishing boats at M'Diq took nerves of steel. Eventually, a thin, worried-looking man in a moth-eaten rowing boat came out to help us. He towed us in, then squeezed us in what looked like an impenetrable corner. The next problem we discovered was filling in all our details at the concrete immigration office behind the fishing wharf. The forms we all had to complete were unbelievably complicated.

'If this is how difficult it is to get into Morocco,' Rosie whispered as we sat hunched round a desk in the rather airless, dingy offices, 'what's it going to be like to get out?'

I wanted to giggle, but decided I'd better not. I was a bit light-headed and still trying to find my land legs after being on the water for so long. What I wanted more than anything was to get the official form-filling over and go out on to the wharf to get some fresh air.

Finally, just as we were congratulating ourselves on successfully completing the immigration forms, José discovered he had to go to the harbour master to fill in more. Then he informed us he had to go to the police inspector's office, to fill out further forms.

'At this rate, all we'll see of Morocco is the harbour,' Alex announced. 'Hey, maybe this is all there is to it anyway.'

Rosie hushed him. 'Do behave. Some people don't have a pronounced sense of humour. So far, I haven't seen anyone smile.'

I glanced about – she was right. Everyone looked decidedly serious and rather morose.

When I looked at Alex, he was studying me. I smiled and he suddenly smiled back.

'Sorry I've acted like an idiot,' he said. 'If I promise

to behave, will you give me some more sailing lessons?'

I laughed, relieved the fight seemed to be over. 'Sure,' I told him.

'Now?' he mouthed, behind his mother's back.

'What?'

'I think I prefer sailing to being stuck around here.' He pulled a face at the bleak surroundings.

I almost took him up on it. The idea of escaping had crossed my mind.

The following morning, after taking in fresh water and taking stock of what new produce we'd need for our trip back to Spain, Alex asked if I'd like to go with him to Tetouan, the former capital of Spanish Morocco.

'The others are going to hire a car, but I thought it would be fun on the local bus. How about it?'

'What about your folks?' I asked.

'They're staying on board – they've been here before. They said it would be all right to ask you.'

'Okay, you're on,' I told him, warming to the idea. 'Give me five minutes to change out of these shorts though.'

'Better wear trousers,' he called after me. 'Otherwise the locals might get shocked seeing such a fantastic pair of bare legs.'

I ignored him, and hurried down to my cabin. After a quick change, I discovered Alex waiting for me on deck.

'Now you do look like a mermaid,' he announced,

brightly. 'Dressed in sea-green, with your sun-streaked hair loose about your shoulders.'

'Will you stop it,' I said.

He held out his hand to steady me as I jumped off the gangplank on to the quay. 'Stop what? Paying you compliments?'

I quickly let go his fingers, and nodded. 'Yes.'

'Why?'

'Because they embarrass me, that's why,' I told him, the old anger threatening.

He gently tugged my hair. 'You are a funny, strange mixture, Susan,' he said. 'Part of growing up is learning to accept compliments. You can't stay a little girl all your life.'

'I don't intend to,' I replied, as I side-stepped to avoid a dirty puddle. I collided with him, and his hands shot out to steady me. For a second I found myself standing in the circle of his arms.

'Will you let me be the first to know when you decide to take the giant step?' he asked, softly. His eyes had a strange tender glow to them.

A tingling began deep inside me and tiny pinpricks of excitement started running up my spine. I felt oddly suspended in time; caught on a faraway star, floating through eternity.

A car hooted loudly, shocking me back to earth. I glanced around. We were standing on a crowded, dirty wharf and had collected an oddly assorted, interested audience.

'Come on, let's catch that bus,' Alex grabbed my hand and pulled me after him. 'Or else I might be arrested for kissing you in public. You never know what the laws are about such things in a foreign country. Mind you, Mum catching us would be just as bad.'

I began to run after him. 'Why should your mother mind?' I called, puzzled.

Alex had sprung on to the creaking running board of the bus and was pulling me up beside him. 'Haven't you twigged her yet?'

I shook my head. 'I don't know what you're getting at?'

We were squeezing inside the crowded bus now, pushed close together, so that Alex's face was touching my hair.

'Mother's quite happy about my light flirtations — but she's always on the lookout to see I don't get serious about a girl. I know for a fact she warns any likely contender off me very early on. I expect she did the same to you.'

The bus jolted and rattled and suddenly lurched forward, throwing me into Alex's arms. I tried to think of what he'd just said about Rosie, but my thoughts were all jumbled. All I could think about was the hardness of his broad chest; the tangy smell of his aftershave and his fingers, on the small of my back . . .

Chapter 10

When we finally arrived back at the *Goddess* and clambered on board, my head was spinning, and my feet ached.

'Lovely, isn't it?' Rosie said, as I sank down on to one of the bank·seats in the saloon.

The picture of the teaming casbah with its baskets of exotic spices, the live chickens and squealing piglets, the secondhand clothes, cross-legged tailors, the bakers with their wares displayed on flat wicker trays, and the metal and leather workers rushed back into my mind.

'It's like looking through a kaleidoscope,' I said. 'Only all those brilliant, coloured patterns are real – people and merchandise . . . I can hardly believe I really saw it, and didn't just dream it all up.'

'Don't forget the pickpockets, either,' Alex remarked.

Rosie shot her son a questioning look. 'Did you get robbed?' she asked. When Alex said no Rosie looked quite relieved.

'It's a big problem,' she said. 'Tourists can be very careless with their possessions.'

'Don't I know it!' Clifford White said as he appeared in the hatchway. 'I should have known better than to leave my wallet in my back pocket. Still, it was only money. Not my credit cards and passport. And there wasn't much cash in it.' His smile rested on me. 'You made quite a stir in the casbah, young lady,' he said, changing the subject.

'Me?' I didn't know what he was getting at.

'Yes, you. I don't think the locals had ever seen such a lovely example of British womanhood – what with your long blonde hair and even longer legs.'

'I wasn't aware of it,' I told him truthfully.

Clifford White nodded, then joined Rosie at the bar and began to pour himself a drink.

'Want something?' he asked, holding up the bottle of vodka.

'She's far too young for that sort of refreshment,' José remarked good-humouredly, 'give her a coke.'

'If you ask me, Susan's too young for a lot of things,' Rosie cut in as she took another sip of Campari.

I felt the tension suddenly fill the cabin and caught the meaningful glance between Alex and his mother.

José must have seen it too because he coughed loudly and slipped an arm round Rosie's waist. 'How about fixing some snacks, cariño?' he suggested.

But I took the cue instead, and walked towards the galley. I wanted some time to myself. I needed to think things through carefully. I liked Rosie, but for some reason – and that reason was obviously Alex – I'd upset her. It seemed it was okay by her for her son to have an endless string of girlfriends, but it was far from being all right for him to have just one. And

Alex, so far had kept her happy – until I'd come on the scene.

I stood in the galley and stared at the fridge. The fact that Rosie had told me the story of Alex's one, two, three tactics to scare me off, seemed obvious now. And it had worked. At first.

But now . . .

'I've come to give you a hand.' Alex interrupted my daydreaming.

I started and self-consciously lent forward to open the fridge.

'Don't pay too much attention to Mother,' Alex whispered as he reached past me and took out the cheese box. 'She'll have to get used to the idea one day.'

I turned to question him. 'Get used to just what, Alex?'

'Why, her little boy growing up,' Alex told me, a grin on his tanned face.

'Is that what it's all about?' I reached for some chorizo, to slice, suddenly happy to have Alex beside me.

'Mainly.' He began cubing some feta cheese but stopped long enough to drop a light kiss on the end of my nose. 'Mothers are like that. You wait until Kevin tells yours about you on this trip.'

'Kevin wouldn't!' I breathed – then saw Alex was laughing. 'Anyway,' I quickly added, 'there's nothing to tell.' I busied myself with the chorizo sausage, but my cheeks were blazing.

'You know,' Alex remarked after a while as we

both made plates of sandwiches, 'Clifford White is absolutely right.'

'About what?' I placed the last piece of paprika sausage on a piece of crusty bread and popped it on to the plate.

'About you being a lovely example of British womanhood,' came the reply.

I turned and faced Alex. 'Do shut up!' I said, smiling.

'That's what I really like about you, Sue. Such a command of your language.' He didn't wait for my reply – which was good in a way!

The four days we spent in Morocco whizzed past and although I loved the exotic atmosphere, the spicy food and different pace of life, I was beginning to miss the excitement and adventure of the open sea.

José plotted our course North, towards the Spanish coast deciding with the Whites where they would like to make for before sailing back to Mallorca.

Marbella seemed to be the popular choice, then to Puerto Banus, and finally across, past Ibiza back to the *Goddess*'s home port.

Shoals of dolphins followed us as we sailed, close hauled for most of the run towards the Spanish coast. The Force Five that had been with us on our outward journey seemed happy to stay with us most of the way. But before we had sighted the pretty and popular marina of Puerto Banus, the wind suddenly dropped and the sails of the *Goddess* emptied and fluttered limply in the still air.

'We'll go in with auxiliary power,' José announced,

when the wind hadn't stirred for several hours. 'We won't lower the sails but try to keep what wind we have forward of the beam. That way, we'll save on fuel.'

I was puzzled, but didn't say anything until later, when José and I were alone.

'Are you worried about how much fuel you've got left?' I asked.

José studied me for a moment, before nodding. 'I don't want the others to know, but as you've worked it out, I'll admit we seem a bit low. Though why, I'll have to check when we reach port.'

'Dad says a ship can save up to twenty per cent on the fuel if you can use motor and sail simultaneously,' I said, hoping to allay his fears.

'Your Dad's right. But the trouble is, will twenty per cent saving be enough to get us safely in?'

'That serious?' I asked. When he didn't reply, I knew it was.

There was a dreamlike quality about the rest of the day, becalmed as we were on the pond-like sea. Under auxiliary motor and with the wind just puffing at the sails, we made hardly any headway. Rosie, and Alice White sunbathed, while the boys occupied themselves with deck games. There was an unreal sense of timelessness – and after a while it began to worry me.

'Take the helm, Susan, while I go below and check our position on the charts,' José said, when I went up to see if he wanted a beer.

'How are we doing?' I asked, my voice low.

José's expression was serious. 'Not too well. I've

had a quick look at the engines – I think there's been a leak in the fuel tank, but where it's going, I daren't think. I might have to switch off altogether. It could be potentially dangerous.'

I stepped up and took the wheel off him. 'What about sending a distress signal over the VHF radio?'

José nodded. 'I think it might come to that if there's no change in the weather by morning.'

I watched him walk to the main hatch, and disappear below decks. For a moment I looked up at the slack sails, then let my gaze run to the horizon. There was nothing but clear, deep blue sea and sky as far as the eye could see.

The sun continued to bake down, shimmering the decks and glancing off the white canvas. Alice and Rosie went below decks, their delight in getting a deeper tan forgotten as the temperature soared.

After a while, even the boys left their games and went below, out of the sun.

When José came aloft to relieve me at the helm, I could see the anxiety lining his rugged features. Obviously, his calculations hadn't done anything to ease his worry.

'We've at least another fifteen miles to cover before land,' he informed me. 'We'll just have to pray the weather changes, but there doesn't seem much hope. I checked.'

'And the engines?'

He shook his head. 'I'm going to have to cut the power before dark. I daren't risk a fire from spillage.'

I didn't speak for the moment, realizing what an impossible position we had found ourselves in.

Drifting on a becalmed sea away from any main shipping lanes, with dead motors, was a skipper's nightmare.

'We'll take turns on the night watches,' I said.

'I couldn't ask you to do that,' José said. But I insisted.

'I'll take my watch, and I think you should tell Alex, too,' I added.

José seemed surprised. 'Why? He's useless at sailing.'

'That's not fair. He's learned a lot this trip. He simply hasn't much confidence but he'll soon find it in an emergency. Basically, he's knowledgeable. He's just never been able to put it into practice.'

José didn't look convinced, but in the end, agreed.

'After all,' he conceded, 'in a situation like this, I guess three sailors are better than two.'

There was an ominous feeling about the *Goddess* after José cut the engines. It seemed all wrong to be in a ship the size of the *Goddess* yet not to be moving. It made me uneasy. But I refused to let my feelings show to any of the others. The last thing we needed was panic.

'Papa has told me we have a small problem.' Alex's face was stern, his lips in a hard line.

I nodded, wondering why he seemed so angry. I soon found out.

'He should have confided in me first,' he said. 'But as usual, he came to me last.'

'Alex,' I said, matching my tone to his, 'this is not the time to start being childish about rights and wrongs. Or who should be told anything first – or last.'

I could see he was about to pounce on me – but his anger suddenly disappeared. He nodded. 'You're right, Susan,' he said, seriously, 'I am very childish sometimes. Mother's quite right to continue to treat me like her little boy when I act like one, I guess.'

His admission made me feel better. More relaxed.

'You are entitled to laugh at me,' he said. 'Sometimes, I could kick myself. You've made me realize many things.' He reached out to lift my ponytail off my shoulder, holding it gently between his fingers. 'I never thought I would ever find a girl who could teach me anything, you know?'

I gently pulled away, swinging my hair back over my shoulders, 'Well, I hope you remember what I've taught you about watching for the direction of the wind, Alex,' I said, 'because you're taking the middle watch.'

'The what watch?'

'It means you're at the helm from midnight till four in the morning.'

For a second a frown creased his forehead. 'You think I could be trusted?'

I had to laugh. 'In this weather, a child could be trusted at the helm.'

'Thanks for that vote of confidence,' he replied. But he was smiling with me.

Something had woken me. In the darkness I lay still for a while trying to fathom out what it was. Then I realized what had woken me. The *Golden Goddess* was moving – pitching up and down – rolling as the water under her ebbed and flowed.

I hadn't bothered to get undressed as I knew I would go back on watch at four.

'What is it?' Rosie asked from her bunk opposite.

'Nothing. Go back to sleep,' I told her. I slipped out of the cabin and crept through the creaking, rolling ship, up on deck.

'I was about to call you,' Alex shouted above the howl of the mounting wind as I joined him in the cockpit.

I looked up at the mainsail, and jib – they were billowing out, pulling and straining. Underneath us, the *Goddess* was quickly gathering speed.

'So much for the weather report,' José stated, appearing beside us under the pale glow of a cloud-shrouded moon.

'What do you want us to do, skipper?' Alex asked, stepping aside and waiting until his father's firm grip had taken over the helm before releasing his own.

'We're going to try and run her into port,' José replied. 'But it means some expert crewing. You up to it?'

Alex looked across at me, and I nodded encouragingly. Then he told his father, 'I'm up to it'.

'Okay. Well Susan, let's get the crew to work, shall we? We can start by letting out that mainsail. We want this wind coming in at right-angles.'

'Aye, aye, skipper!' I called, then started forward, Alex right behind me. 'Remember what I taught you about a ship running,' I shouted above the rising wind.

'We have to keep the wind coming in from one quarter of the transom, right?' Alex surprised me.

'Right!' I shouted back. 'If the wind should ever get behind the mainsail the whole sail could crash over from one side of the boat to the other.

'And accidental gybe, isn't that what you called it?'

I could have hugged him if my hands hadn't been clinging desperately on to the wet lifelines.

'Right again. The last thing we need now is to dismast the ship.'

'Before you two move another step, you go and put your life-jackets on,' José commanded us.

I waved that I'd understood, then shouted to Alex who was now ahead of me. I felt a bit embarrassed. Wearing life-jackets is another of Dad's laws – and I'd been so intent on instructing Alex that I'd let it slip out of my mind.

The rest of the night and well into the dawn, we battled to keep the *Goddess* ahead of the storm. Then, at last, as the first grey fingers of morning streaked through the dark clouds, the wind began to drop. During the long hours of running before the sudden storm, Clifford and the boys had come up on deck to help. Between us, the *Golden Goddess* had really come out tops. She was a magnificent ship. Strong – like a panther straining at its leash to ride out the elements. Powerful. Proud and masterful. I loved every inch of her.

Chapter 11

I must have fallen asleep as soon as we were safely berthed. It was well after ten before I heard a movement in the cabin. I rolled over, peering through bleary eyes.

For a moment, all I could see was a mass of pink roses. I'm still dreaming, I thought, and was about to roll back on to my tummy to go to sleep again, when Rosie laughed.

'Hey! These are for you, Susan,' she said, appearing from behind the bouquet like a pixie over the top of a toadstool.

She plonked the flowers unceremoniously on my tummy then sat on my bunk.

I sat up, still confused. 'It's not my birthday,' I said, tracing one of the perfect blooms with my fingers.

'These are a collective thank you from the rest of the *Goddess*'s crew,' she informed me. Then said, 'Now, get up and get dressed, we're all going into Marbella. We'll shop, go to the hairdresser's, and generally rehumanize ourselves.'

'What about the engines?' I asked.

Rosie scowled. 'What about them?'

'Didn't José tell you?' I could see from her

continued confusion that he hadn't, and could have kicked myself.

'Is there something wrong with them? Is that it?' She narrowed her gaze at me. 'I thought his expansive plans for our comfort was out of the goodness of his heart, and all the time he wanted us out of the way so that he could get the engines looked at!'

'Please, Rosie, don't say anything,' I said. 'He didn't want anyone worried unduly, that's all.'

'And what about you? A kid as young as you *can* be worried, is that it?'

'I'm not a kid, Rosie,' I said. 'I know I've still got a lot of growing up to do, but I'm not a kid. Nor is Alex—' I stopped abruptly, wondering if I'd said too much. We stared at each other without speaking for a while and then I shrugged. 'Sorry.'

She shook her red curls, smiling wistfully. 'Do you know, Alex said the same thing to me this morning?'

'He did?' The idea excited me. I began to feel all warm and marshmallowy inside.

Standing up, she walked to the door. 'If I didn't think I was being an old romantic, I'd go as far as to say my horrible, handsome son's gone overboard.'

I laughed happily thinking that was a pretty apt description of how I felt about him. Not that I planned telling him. Not for a while. We still had to get back home and dry to port. And that was another week away. Maybe another week at sea with him would change my mind? Somehow, I doubted it.

Rosie squeezed my hand. She didn't say anything more.

*

Andraitx harbour appeared like a pair of welcoming arms as we cut the Goddess's repaired motors and began to take her into port under sail.

'That looks like a welcoming committee,' Alex said, pointing to a collection of people waving to us from the quay.

'I should hope it is!' Rosie said. She stood on the bow and began to wave back. 'I did telephone them from Puerto Banus to say exactly when to expect us.'

'What if the wind had dropped again?' José asked.

But Rosie wasn't in the mood for bantering. She was far too excited at the prospect of getting ashore.

'Will you be crewing on the Goddess next year?' Mark asked, as we tied up.

I smiled apologetically. 'Can't really say, Mark,' I told him. Then asked, 'Why?'

He shrugged a bit self-consciously, and shuffled his feet. 'Well, it would be nice to see you again. You're a cracking good sailor.'

I nearly laughed out loud. It was the nearest thing to a compliment that I'd had in a long time – well, since Alex had held me in his arms in the moonlight and told me I was a very special type of girl. I felt my cheeks growing hot as I remembered and busied myself with coiling a rope.

I was aware of Mark standing awkwardly in front of me still, and blinked up at him against the brilliant sunlight.

He was smiling at me shyly. 'Well, goodbye then,' he stammered. Then he stooped and aimed a moist, hesitant kiss at my mouth. Only the boat moved and he missed. He kissed my ear instead.

I smiled up at him. 'Thank you for that,' I said kindly. 'You're a really nice boy, Mark – and you're going to be a great sailor too.'

'And you're the best girl I've ever met!' Mark blurted out before he turned to run down the gangplank.

I heard Alex tut-tut from behind me. 'Poor young lad,' he patronized. 'It must be terrible to lose the first girl you fall for to a bloke as handsome, intelligent and charming as me.'

I spun round, about to tell him some home truths. Such as, he was big-headed, self-opinionated, egotistical – oh, and a load of other nasties – but I didn't, because I was suddenly gazing into a pair of deep, taunting eyes; and a pair of strong arms were being wrapped round me. The next second, a pair of soft, warm lips covered mine. . . .

A loud cheering and cat-calling shattered my very first, purely magical moment. Embarrassed, I pulled away from Alex.

'I thought you were all against shipboard romances?' Kevin called, playfully, from where he stood, his arm round Pilar, on the quay.

I laughed back. 'I still am!'

'Then what was all that about just now?'

'That, dear brother, was what is generally known as practising the kiss of life. It's all part of the lessons I've been giving Alex.'

Alex chortled. 'You know, I don't think I quite got it right,' he said, reaching out to grab me again.

But I ducked, and ran quickly down the gangplank to join the others.

I was still laughing as we all walked, arm-in-arm, up to the club house.

'Are you going to continue to play hard to get?' Alex asked, catching me up and slipping a possessive arm round my waist. His fingers felt firm and warm through my thin cotton T-shirt. I felt all at once happy and excited and yet strangely nervous.

'Not so much hard to get as just taking things slowly Alex,' I said, glancing up at him. He was smiling down at me with a secret, tender expression in his eyes. Gone were all the flashing, teasing glances, the sardonic amusement – and in their place there was an intimacy which made my heart begin to hammer against my ribs. It was all so new and unnerving. To be honest, I felt safer riding through the eye of a storm than I felt with Alex so close to me at that moment. A shiver involuntarily ran through me and feeling it, Alex held me closer.

I might be a better sailor, I thought, but when it comes to falling in love, I'm out of my depth.

As if reading my thoughts, Alex grinned and dropped a light kiss on my neck. I pushed him away and glowered.

'Don't do that!' I hissed, hoping no one else had noticed.

No one had – they'd all gone into the club house!

Overhead, a seagull soared into the arc of blue sky and I laughed at its antics as it flew higher and higher It was so alive. Free. Vibrant.

'I think I love you, Susan,' Alex was saying. And I was smiling at him and then looking up again at the seagull – just a speck now, high in the azure sky. And I laughed happily. If this was love, it was incredible. Wonderful. Exhilarating.

But I didn't want to examine it too closely. Not yet awhile. I just wanted to be like that seagull – and fly on the wings of it. That was enough for now.

More than enough because somehow I knew I would never want to come down to earth again. How could I, when I was flying so high?